FROM THE SHADOWS

Edited By Donna Samworth

Years of

First published in Great Britain in 2020 by:

YoungWriters®
— Est. 1991 —

Young Writers
Remus House
Coltsfoot Drive
Peterborough
PE2 9BF
Telephone: 01733 890066
Website: www.youngwriters.co.uk

Printed and bound in the UK by BookPrintingUK
Website: www.bookprintinguk.com
YB0452G

FORELUORD

Enter, Reader, if you dare...

For as long as there have been stories there have been
ghost stories. Writers have been trying scare their readers
for centuries using just the power of their imagination. For
Young Writers' latest competition Spine-Chillers we asked
pupils to come up with their own spooky tales, but with the
tricky twist of using just 100 words!

They rose to the challenge magnificently and this resulting
collection of haunting tales will certainly give you the creeps!
From friendly ghosts and Halloween adventures to the
gruesome and macabre, the young writers in this anthology
showcase their creative writing talents.

Here at Young Writers our aim is to encourage creativity and
to inspire a love of the written word, so it's great to get such
an amazing response, with some absolutely fantastic stories.

I'd like to congratulate all the young authors in this collection
- I hope this inspires them to continue with their creative
writing. And who knows, maybe we'll be seeing their names
alongside Stephen King on the best seller lists in the future...

CONTENTS

EPSOM COLLEGE, EPSOM

Esme Jordan (12)   52

HIGHCLIFFE SCHOOL, HIGHCLIFFE

Hannah Foy (13)	53
Jack Davis (13)	54
Sophie Donaldson (13)	55
Harriet Jones (12)	56
Harrison Parker (12)	57
Amelia Laryea (13)	58
Toby Staddon (13)	59
Tayla Hewitt (12)	60
Moses Harry (13)	61
Scarlett Adams (13)	62
Ben Aldred (14)	63
Bel Bartlett (13)	64
Millie Musker (12)	65
Harper Scotford (13)	66
Jessica Hefferan (13)	67
Logan Smith (13)	68
Jonah Sargent (12)	69

KENSINGTON PARK SCHOOL, LONDON

Zara Latif (12)	70
Henry Thornton (12)	71
Marilena Bors (12)	72
Millie McDonald (12)	73
Kitty Kinsman (12)	74

MAIDSTONE GRAMMAR SCHOOL, MAIDSTONE

Thomas Whentringhame (16)	75
Jack Whentringhame (16)	76

NEWLAND HOUSE SCHOOL, TWICKENHAM

Oliver La Torre	77
Ben Harris	78
Blake Haden (13)	79

Miles Bell (13)	80
Tim Wright (13)	81
Dimitri Tzinieris	82
James G-S	83
Edward Knott	84
Dylan Grewal (12)	85

NIGHTINGALE COMMUNITY ACADEMY, TOOTING

Tasian Thomas (11)	86
Jaylen South (12)	87
Yahya Kamal (11)	88
Brandon Page (12)	89

RADNOR HOUSE SEVENOAKS SCHOOL, SUNDRIDGE

Chloe Perversi (15)	90
James Hori (13)	91
Tilly Beckerman (12)	92
Charlie Paye (13)	93
Iona Day (13)	94
Max Harrison (13)	95
Matilda Simons (11)	96
Isobel King (14)	97
Edward Shilling (14)	98
Charlotte Flenghi (13)	99
Josh Hassan (12)	100
Alice Munn (11)	101
Will Smith (13)	102

SIR ROBERT PATTINSON ACADEMY, NORTH HYKEHAM

Lewis Merryweather (13)	103
Matthew Rowe (11)	104
Lewis Kirk (12)	105
Rosie Wilkins (12)	106
Isabella Kerrison (12)	107
Logan Edward Wakefield (13)	108
Phoebe Hardie (11)	109
Thomas Dickinson (12)	110
Callum Fields (13)	111

SMESTOW SCHOOL, CASTLECROFT

Rebecca Ball	112
Georgie Hooper (11)	113
Eve Stairmand-Jackson	114
Jasleen Kaur (13)	115

ST DAVID'S COLLEGE, LLANDUDNO

Olivia Goodwin (12)	116
Jacob Wilkinson (11)	117
Jack Kennedy (12)	118

ST JOHN'S CATHOLIC COMPREHENSIVE SCHOOL, GRAVESEND

Rebecca Sales (12)	119
Emeka Esenwa (14)	120
Stephanie Kingsland (12)	121
Bianka Latka (12)	122

ST JULIE'S CATHOLIC HIGH SCHOOL, WOOLTON

Jessica Ryan (12)	123
Evie Roberts (12)	124
Rosie Ali Mohammed (12)	125
Christelle Eve Bwaka (12)	126
Cerys Davies (11)	127
Shona Shaji (12)	128
Amelia Boyle (12)	129
Amelia Jones (12)	130
Filipa Caixinha (12)	131

THE BISHOP OF LLANDAFF CIW HIGH SCHOOL, CARDIFF

Jason Wei (12)	132
Polly Hoade (13)	133

THE GATWICK SCHOOL, CRAWLEY

Daniel Dantas Sa (11)	134
Carys Cresswell (12)	135
Isabella Seelig (12)	136
Leo Harwood-Duffy (12)	137
Elise Grace-Hills (13)	138
Harrison James Bamforth (11)	139
Eleanor Allard (12)	140
Casey Burgar (13)	141
Hope Phelps (12)	142
Kerys Barrow (11)	143
Roheyatou Jagana (12)	144
Xanthe Valentine (14)	145
Harry Smith (13)	146
Daisy Hitchcock (13)	147
Paige Smith (11)	148
Paige Newman (12)	149
Amberjeet Panesar (12)	150
Annie Mae Hitchcock (15)	151
Katie Willimott (12)	152
Jessica Gurr (15)	153
Louise Cannon (11)	154
Chenai Vusani (15)	155
Zahra Mahmood (15)	156
Caitlin Trigwell (12)	157
Thomas Stagg (14)	158
Pippa Watts (12)	159
Rochelle Barrow (15)	160
Lucy Munday (12)	161
Aamani Parekh (14)	162
David Mihai (13)	163
Eloise Maan (13)	164
Kimora Kanjanda (11)	165
Jessica Mary-Anne Cooke (11)	166
Carolina Santana (14)	167
Jessica Fiyinfoluwa Fawole (13)	168
Manuela Raimundo (12)	169
Harry Feild (14)	170
Harriet Watts (11)	171
Cole Scott (13)	172
James Ruby (13)	173
Rose Waller (12)	174
Tilly Astley (11)	175
Tatiana Almeida (13)	176

THE MINI SAGAS

SATANIC SOULS ARISE

Dim and unilluminated weren't enough to describe the constricted diminutive room. My senses were alerting me that people were in the vicinity of me. My head whizzed checking for obstacles. Unexpectedly, I heard a grotesque shriek. Moments later, I heard the same yell. I wanted to convince myself to look but couldn't make a glimpse in the darkness. Unaware of consequences, I decided to track down the horrific sound, strolling over that direction. Someone then laid a crushing hand on me. I kicked the air, luckily killing someone, the so-called 'Satan'. Dim and unilluminated are currently still not enough.

PHARRELL LUSINDE

HUNTED

Tip-tap! Pitter-patter! A scavenger passed through the serpentine limbs of trees. Pretty, pink coloured ears arched back in alarm, sensing the rustle, hustle of its giver of death. Athletic legs of the rabbit remain in a brisk sprint, nettles and nature alike whizzing past within an emerald haze. Her sense of alarm heightened, paranoia filling her every hop, every dodge. Amber fur danced in the greenery, paws pacing towards their target. Suffering had announced itself now. She'd run too long. A grin surpassed and teeth bared, snarling as he knew when to strike. One pace. Two pace... Prance.

SOPHIE JOBES

CRUCIO

Walking down the long desolate Bryant street, an owl swooped down onto my shoulder and put out its leg, revealing a slip of parchment with an address. Knowing that someone was murdered, I hurried to the address. As I arrived the family were up like nothing happened. Suddenly, the man pulled out his wand and cried, "Crucio!" It was agony like none other. As I was released, I grabbed my own wand and shouted, "Expelliarmus!" to disarm the family. The minister for magic, Cornelius Fudge, arrived and sentenced the family to fifteen years with the Dementors in Azkaban.

DAVID KELLY (16)

THE SHADOW SERIAL KILLER

In the year 1996, it lay in shadows. It was something unthinkable. As it came out of the night, millions would try catching it but all that was seen was dimness, that lured in its prey.
One night, two boys set out in the gloom. Later they slept, one woke and heard a howl. He saw the shadow of something's tail, as it got bigger... and bigger... and closer and closer. He looked behind and his friend was gone. He then turned back to see its shadow, but it wasn't there. A bang sounded. He lost consciousness...

LIAM MYATT

MY EYES DECEIVE ME

You think you know someone, years of treachery lies and deceit. I loved her, but to her I was merely an object, an item in her schemes. I fell in love with an alias, an alias of a demonic psychopath who relishes in other people's pain. I was another hopeless fool destined for love that ended in heartbreak. I lost my family, friends, and my self respect. I can no longer look in the mirror and not feel shameful of my foolishness. And as a result I now carry the weight of the guilt, the guilt of aiding a murder.

HOLLIE DRAPER (13)

PRISON BREAK

I couldn't run for much longer, but luckily I got home. I looked out the window and there he was, standing there in the bushes. For one second, I looked away. He was even closer! I locked all the doors and windows, but suddenly, I heard a bang. I looked downstairs and I saw him lurking in the shadows. His red eyes were glowing and he had sharp nails. I saw him again, this time dragging a bag. I went to hide in the closet. I went to look behind me. There he was, just standing there...

AMAN KOROTANIA

DON'T KILL YOUR TEACHER

Do you get that feeling? That feeling when a chill runs down your spine. I do, and it's because right now, I'm standing in a cemetery with my friend. It gets worse. He accidentally murdered the principal, so he's burying him. After he buries the corpse, we go home. I soon drift off to sleep.
When I wake, I go to my friend's house. I am petrified at what I see. I see my friend, dead on the floor, with staples through his heart and that's how the principal died! Is the principal still alive? That's impossible. He's dead...

LIAM STARES (12)
Alec Hunter Academy, Braintree

THE VOICE

It was late at night, I was walking home. As I walked I could hear a voice, it eerily whispered, "Joooossssssshhhhhhhh!" That voice was coming from the graveyard. I entered and saw a church. As I moved closer, the whispering voice became clearer, louder and more spine-chilling. Suddenly it stopped. I was standing inside the old church. Then out of nowhere, that eerie voice muttered, "I can see you, do you want to see me?" I pretended not to be scared. I saw him staring at me. I froze with fear. He sneered, "I can make accidents happen you know..."

JOSHUA ARMSTRONG (12)

Cantonian High School, Llandaff

Umbrella Girl

The man ran and ran until his legs gave way, he tripped on a sharp rock and fell hard onto the floor. Following swiftly behind him was a young girl with piercing dark eyes, holding an umbrella, ready to strike. He clambered to his feet and ran. He ran for his life! His heart was racing, time slowed, his hair stood on end... he was terrified! With one strike, she lunged forward and this time he couldn't escape!
The following morning, police were examining a body, he had been found, umbrella still protruding from his heart!
Who was the girl?

Lily Barratt (12)
Cantonian High School, Llandaff

Haunted Organ

It was a jet-black night. The wind was howling like a wolf, the trees were shivering as if they were cold. I walked warily into the churchyard, all I could see into the darkness were the morbid gravestones. I knew that the church was haunted by a rogue, restless spirit. This made me feel sick with dread as I crept closer to the church. I entered, it felt cold and damp. I felt faint, I wanted to run back out through the rusty church doors. I walked further inside, my heart pounding. Suddenly the organ began to play...

Sam Bragg (12)
Cantonian High School, Llandaff

THE HUNTED SITAR

One month ago, I was an archaeologist known as Derek Hood. I was studying ancient artefacts of India. I saw a marble-coloured building called the Taj Mahal. It was very huge and shiny. Me and the rest of the team went inside. While I was resting, as I put my hand on the wall, it moved and I slid down. Once I slid down I heard a voice saying, "Come to me!" The voice was coming from the sitar. Then I touched it and mysterious powers were flooding into me. And then, I was the Zarrter...

MAX CULLIFORD (13)
Cantonian High School, Llandaff

UNRESPONSIVE

"I've really messed up this time. I wonder how I'm going to get treated after this." He couldn't keep staring at his hands. His sister was lying on a bench, sleeping. Whenever people walked by him, they kept screaming and running, knowing that something was wrong. "Hello, Lucy?" Lucy was unresponsive, still in her sleep. A voice in his head was talking to him: "You did this, not me, you're to blame, this is all you!" It keeps talking and talking. He was going insane, screaming and licking off the blood of his hands. Lucy was still unresponsive. "Help me!"

EXAUCE MALULA (12)
Cardinal Newman Catholic School, Coventry

INFECTED

A strange feeling's been burdening me for a few days now. I'll suddenly have an immense eruption of energy but then experience vast fatigue. The relentless work, countless consultations and increased surgical demand have taken a toll.

Exhausted, I lie motionless on the office sofa when an infuriating itch apprehends my arm. Minutes pass and the pain becomes unbearable. Alarmed, I inspect my arm to be met by a horrifying sight: black ink running up my arm painting my veins, around what looked like a worm under my skin. My muscle seizes and spasms, allowing dozens more to reveal themselves...

OCEAN WHITE (14)
Cardinal Newman Catholic School, Coventry

FOOTSTEPS TO FEAR

Halloween, full of excitement and scares. Jamie had gone trick or treating with his friends to the scary mansion on the isolated hilltop. It was an unusual stormy night with flashing throughout the sky. On approaching, they heard knocking on the door. Jamie bravely walked inside on the creaky floorboards. He started to hear moaning, Jamie's heart was beating as fast as a cheetah. He went up the winding staircase to the ajar door, peeked inside and terror ran through his body at what he saw. At lightning speed, Jamie ran to his friends screaming, "Monsters!" What were they?

HOLLY TAYLOR (11)
Cardinal Newman Catholic School, Coventry

DARKNESS

The anointed Lord of the Realm held his breath, frozen as stone, except his trembling jaw. Staring. Waiting. He'd travelled far to get here, leaving a world of demons. Now the only survivor of his land. Shadows danced around him, reminding him of happier times. These lights, however, were flickering torches, trying to locate him before he could find her. He rested his eyes on his glistening silver sword. Ready. A creak of a floorboard. The handle turned and rattled. The candle flared brightly and then went out, with a quiet hiss. He was surrounded by darkness. Darkness... Silence...

KYMANI CRUZ (11)

Cardinal Newman Catholic School, Coventry

THE HOUSE

I crept into the abandoned, derelict house not knowing what to expect. Me and my friend were going to meet in there, so I waited a few minutes. Ten minutes. Twenty minutes. Thirty minutes. I couldn't wait any longer. So, I flicked on the torch eagerly and explored. Walking past the cracked, broken walls. Sneaking across the creaky, damaged, rotten wooden floor. I went past many deceased, withered plants. There were strange paintings, it felt like they had eyes and were watching my every move. I heard the door creak open. "Jake?" I asked. A cold hand covered my mouth...

AVA WHITTLE (11)

Cardinal Newman Catholic School, Coventry

GAME OVER

The girl sits in front of the screen watching it intensely, this is it. Carefully observing the pixels on the TV screen, she moves her avatar left and right, avoiding the onslaught of raining rocks and creatures. It's getting harder now, there's more things raining from the top of the screen, explosions going off and lasers shooting. There's nowhere to run, they're coming closer now, they're above, in front and behind. Stuck. And just like that, the girl collapses, slumping like a rag doll in front of the screen that now projects the words: *Game Over.*

EMILY SUCHANSKA (13)
Cardinal Newman Catholic School, Coventry

THE GRASP!

Sweat trickled down my back. I knew I wouldn't make it back by dark. I saw an old, abandoned house. The grass was as tall as me, with little life inside it. *I'll go in there and call Chloe...* at least that's what I thought. I tried to turn my phone on, it was dead! Lightning struck the top of the house like in the movie 'Frankenstein' when they experimented on him. I managed to grasp my way through the smashed window. "Hello?" No answer. Moonlight shone through the smashed window onto something strange. A cold hand grabbed my shoulder...

LIBBY COX (13)

Cardinal Newman Catholic School, Coventry

A BLOOD-CURDLING NIGHT'S DREAM

"Help, help." I looked out my window with the torrential rain falling at the boy's feet. He sprinted into my home and remarked worriedly, "There is a clown hunting me... I turned the corner and lost him. Help me please."
I responded, "Did he look like this?" I transmuted into the clown that was chasing him moments later. He shrieked like a banshee. I chased him round the house. He was a frightened little girl. The coat that was drowning him was on the floor, trapping him... I consumed children. I seized him, tearing him to shreds.

FAYE TAYLOR (12)
Cardinal Newman Catholic School, Coventry

DISAPPEARED

Sitting in the back seat of my dad's car, I listen to my favourite music while I await his return. My head deep into my phone, the car door opens. "Hey, Dad." Surprisingly, there is no reply from him. Gazing up out of my phone. My heart ceases. That's not my dad! "Sir, I think you have the wrong car." Sweat trickles down my back, palms clammy, heart pounding. He's silent. Edging towards the car door, I tug on it. *Click.* He slowly turns round and stares at me, frowning. Shaking his head, he lunges towards me. All goes black.

ABBEY TAYLOR (14)
Cardinal Newman Catholic School, Coventry

DEATH'S CALLING

Walking down the road, I stopped. There was a shadow in front of me, overlooking the pavement. I looked to my left and there was nobody, to my right only a lamp post? As I slowly ambled further towards my house there was a sudden calling and gust of wind from behind. Darting round, there was nothing. Another voice cried out, "Johnny." I began to pace faster along the street and my house was in sight. Again they exclaimed "Johnny" in a slow voice. There was nobody for miles around, who could it be? Then, heavy breathing penetrated my soul...

DUNCAN MOYNIHAN (13)
Cardinal Newman Catholic School, Coventry

THE HOUSE

The house had an eerie aura to it. It had been abandoned for hundreds of years. All the windows of the house were shattered. He walked inside, the musty yellow walls were covered in stains. The rotten green wood was cracked and was letting out a disgusting smell. The doors were scattered along the floor and the furniture was gone... All except for a clock. A ticking clock. A clock that was too modern for the house. He heard the floorboards creak behind him. A long wrinkly arm curled and grasped the doorway and whispered, "I knew you would come..."

LIAM DOWSE (13)
Cardinal Newman Catholic School, Coventry

THE PLUNGE

I acknowledged my floating residence may not survive the night. Shimmering shards of water paralysed me, glistening in the light radiated from the moon as our metal exterior creaked under the pressure. I had nowhere to go... nowhere to hide... nowhere to run... We were minute compared to the power engulfing our position, as their primary weapon - something as common as the liquid we drink - seeped through the flaws in our defences. We were being toyed with, our vessel so small to the depths of the ocean. Reaching for my radio, I took a breath and dived...

ANDREW MCELROY (14)

Cardinal Newman Catholic School, Coventry

REGRET

Everything is dark and cold and I can't feel anything. I can't move, can't see, can't breathe. The warm and damp air in here is scarce, practically suffocating me. Now there's an agonising, icy pain coursing through my body, shocking me back to my grim reality. Up above, I can hear quiet, muffled voices; some people are sobbing, others are muttering to themselves. I want to cry, I want to scream - but I can't. I just want to get out of here, it was a mistake from the beginning... I knew I should've asked to be cremated instead.

LOLITA TOMSCHEY-CARTER (13)
Cardinal Newman Catholic School, Coventry

THE ABNORMALITY

It was a murky, stormy night and a girl named Lucy, with her friends Jason and Laura, were heading home after a long night of partying. Suddenly, Laura had a sudden urge to go to the toilet.

Jason said, "Are you serious?!"

As they stopped off at the nearby gas station, Laura got out of the car and ran to the toilets. Jason and Lucy then heard a piercing shriek coming from the station.

"Go!" shouted Lucy.

As they sped off they saw Laura running towards the car, then someone snatched her and there was an explosion of blood.

ALETHEA KIANSUNGUA (12)
Cardinal Newman Catholic School, Coventry

KIDNAPPED BY MY STALKER

I woke up to the smell of chicken. This wasn't my house because I'm vegan, I don't eat chicken even though my room was the exact same.

A few minutes later, I found myself going down the creaky stairs and entering the kitchen following the stronger smell of chicken. Out of nowhere, I saw a tall figure turned around to face me, he was holding a butcher knife right next to my chest.

I woke up, panicked and heavily breathing. I rushed to my window in shock from my nightmare and saw him standing outside, looking straight into my bedroom...

COURTNEY BLACKBIRD-THOMSON (12)

Cardinal Newman Catholic School, Coventry

THE LAST BREATH

I crept into the dusty house; adrenaline running high. I could sense everyone else was feeling the same. As I looked on top of the staircase, there stood a man in white, tears of blood pouring down his face. Mandy made the mistake of racing towards him... Within seconds she was the first to die. People began to notice in a nearby painting, bloody tears running down her face. I went cold. Everyone began screaming and ran off in different directions, the same happening to them. I felt myself taking my last breath... before my life came to an end.

GWENETH KIASUNGUA (12)

Cardinal Newman Catholic School, Coventry

THE LOST WOMAN

As I entered the house with my two friends, Amelia and Ava, there was a loud noise in the corridor and we didn't want to go there. Ava spoke and said, "If we want to know who never left this house, we need to go further." We agreed and went further into the house. As quiet as possible the three of us went inside the bedroom, then the door shut and locked. We started to panic...

"Hello?" No answer. We sat on the bed and held each other tight.

Bang! A breeze passed and whispered, "Girls..."

ADRIANA MACHALA (12)

Cardinal Newman Catholic School, Coventry

THE PERFECT CHILD

"Atishoo!" I scrunch up my nose as I apply the pink blush to my new child. Critically admiring my work, now just a nose. Slowly I stand up and step over all the mangled bodies on the floor, each one with a different body part missing. I scan over the bodies, judging all of them. Eventually I decide on a small button nose attached to a fragile child, now sprawled over a patch of blood. Carefully I cut off the nose and start to sew it onto my child.

"You'll be the perfect child, soon," I assure her lifeless body.

POPPY O'KEEFFE (14)
Cardinal Newman Catholic School, Coventry

THAT HALLOWEEN NIGHT...

It was the night of Halloween. We knew there was no turning back. The gates creaked open as lightning lit up the night sky. *Tick-tock, tick-tock,* I heard as I entered the house. This house had been abandoned for over a century now, but somehow it all seemed alive. Sweat trickled down my spine as I walked down the stairs to the basement. I felt like someone was watching me. I took a deep breath and lit a candle. Everything beyond the circle of light seemed creepy and frightening. Then I saw it. The diary of Thomas Rodriguez...

OLIWIA LUSZCZ (12)
Cardinal Newman Catholic School, Coventry

THE PERFECT CHILD

"Atishoo!" I scrunch up my nose as I apply the pink blush to my new child. Critically admiring my work, now just a nose. Slowly I stand up and step over all the mangled bodies on the floor, each one with a different body part missing. I scan over the bodies, judging all of them. Eventually I decide on a small button nose attached to a fragile child, now sprawled over a patch of blood. Carefully I cut off the nose and start to sew it onto my child.

"You'll be the perfect child, soon," I assure her lifeless body.

POPPY O'KEEFFE (14)

Cardinal Newman Catholic School, Coventry

THAT HALLOWEEN NIGHT...

It was the night of Halloween. We knew there was no turning back. The gates creaked open as lightning lit up the night sky. *Tick-tock, tick-tock,* I heard as I entered the house. This house had been abandoned for over a century now, but somehow it all seemed alive. Sweat trickled down my spine as I walked down the stairs to the basement. I felt like someone was watching me. I took a deep breath and lit a candle. Everything beyond the circle of light seemed creepy and frightening. Then I saw it. The diary of Thomas Rodriguez...

OLIWIA LUSZCZ (12)

Cardinal Newman Catholic School, Coventry

YOU'LL BE SAFER WITH IT

I was still crying about everything. I didn't know how to move on. 'It protects you' they say until it takes that one irreplaceable thing from you. I heard a voice, a voice so familiar. I followed it, it led to a trail of deep red. Cautiously I raised my head, then I saw it, the cause of my aggravating pain. I observed its rigid and excruciating imperfections. And I saw something more, something deeper; it was like an army of trapped people. I looked further to realise the people were advancing to form the name of... me!

TENDAYI MPHO CHIGWADA (14)
Cardinal Newman Catholic School, Coventry

THE KEEPER

I sprinted towards the door, hoping I could lose him. *Slam!* I made it. It was because of this laptop, I wish I'd never stolen it. I had to sell it but something was on it worth killing for. My pulse quickened and raced. I felt throbbing through my temples. It was silent. I heard footsteps and saw a shadow under the door. I held my breath and panicked; I needed to escape. All I could hear was our breathing. Patiently, I waited for an opening to escape. All of a sudden, I spotted a window and a hammer. *Smash...*

RISHE SEKAR (14)
Cardinal Newman Catholic School, Coventry

Do As I Say

A normal night, 'Death Note' on the TV, close to sleeping, when the screen made a weird screech and crackle. A face came up, the only words he screeched out were, "Do as I say!" I felt something dig into my hand, a small TEC-9. My phone beeped, it read: 'Go on a rampage - no armour, just the gun'. I ran away and hid, I couldn't do it. Then I started to hear some eerie music out of a horror movie. A few footsteps, then that face I saw reappeared... "Time to die!" were the last words I heard.

JACK JEGANATHAN (12)

Cardinal Newman Catholic School, Coventry

SAFETY FIRST

As I ran towards the building's entrance, I happened to wonder if he was still there. Clutching my now red dripping hand I paced steadily towards what I thought was to be a sanctuary. The closer I got the less there was pain. The want for safety sent me berserk trying everything to reach this ethereal place. Running, I looked back for reassurance to see the black outline in a blackened place. It was it. It squealed in rage and charged at what seemed to be me. Its overalls of fur, black and unpleasant. Was I going to make it?

MICHAL BART DRZEWINSKI (14)

Cardinal Newman Catholic School, Coventry

The Well Of Souls

The disappearances were now a weekly thing. On Sage Grove people were vanishing without a trace. Not many people cared about them. They would not at all be missed. For while they lived on that road their souls were being taken. Maybe they were even giving them away but the only thing that connected the street was the well. They would all put a coin in and make a wish. Some would wish harder than others but they all wished for the same thing: happiness. For while they lived on that street the well would slowly take their souls...

Milly Bennell-Low (13)
Cardinal Newman Catholic School, Coventry

THE FOREST

Jackson was in the forest. A dark, foggy forest. He had no recollection of how he had got there except something told him that he was being chased. Without a second thought, his legs scrambled away from the spot he was standing on. Jackson ran for what felt like an hour, until he stumbled upon a house. A simple wooden cottage. Should he go in? A growl came from the distance behind him. Without thinking he ran in and hid in the nearest wardrobe. He was shivering. He heard the door swing open with a bang. Then... he woke up!

MADELEINE HINE (12)

Cardinal Newman Catholic School, Coventry

THE DEMON BEHIND ME

I look into the mirror and there he is, standing behind me as I touch up my make-up. Later he's smirking and hunched over in the passenger seat. Spitting on a passing student, the demon gets out of the car. Running his claws over the Mercedes' logo, he stomps along behind me. A mean grin plastered on his face, he shouts at any student remotely confused, incorrect or upset. He won't go away. He follows me everywhere. I can't get rid of him. I hate him with every bone in my body. But how can I? He's me.

MATTI ARMSTON (13)
Cardinal Newman Catholic School, Coventry

Nightmare Or Not?

Sweat trickled down my back, I looked around at the people circling at an impossible speed. Where was I? What should I do? As I looked up I saw... "Argh! Woah!" I could not see anything. As I pulled my attention to the dark evil clouds, I saw... my mum! I was shaking like crazy. I could hear people screaming inside my head. Demons still circling around I could smell a sense of panic and confusion. As sweat poured from me like tears I was shouting out, "Mum, is that you?" as fear engulfed me...

Abigail Thompson (12)

Cardinal Newman Catholic School, Coventry

THE NEW HOUSE

There is a new house which has just appeared out of nowhere. Everyone is too scared to enter but it's just a house so I shall go towards this house of devouring brightness like a possible heaven, however, it has a ring to it. When you open the door only the birds can be heard. Looking around it looks fully functional. The only problem is that the rooms seem to be moving! Now I feel bewildered. Is this just a joke? Why has this room become full of mirrors? Wait a minute, why are there massive crowds? Oh no...!

ADAM JACKSON (14)
Cardinal Newman Catholic School, Coventry

IS IT? IT CAN'T BE!

Goosebumps were popping out of my body... I was at my best friend Sam's funeral. He was in a car crash and was the only one that didn't survive. My mum didn't want to attend his funeral but of course I still did. I was left in a dark room, cobwebs everywhere with no windows and not a single soul in sight. I was trying to look around to find a way out but I started hearing noises. I tried to get away from it but it got closer. Then a cold hand touched mine. "Sam... it can't be you..."

MADISON DAVIES (15)

Cardinal Newman Catholic School, Coventry

SPINE-CHILLING TALE

Night cold, darkness piercing the air like a knife through skin. Tears flowing from my eyes desperately. The only things visible slowly disappearing. As I look down I see the blade. Streams of blood oozes out of my wound, life exiting my body, ready to leave a corpse behind. As my friends shriek in fear I can see the anxiety in their eyes. Next thing I know I'm being lifted into an ambulance. My mum and friends gazing at me, perturbation engulfing them. What is that? Is my life finished for good?

VINNIE DARBY (14)

Cardinal Newman Catholic School, Coventry

PANDEMONIUM

The floorboards creaked, the windows leaked... *drip-drop, drip-drop*...There it was again, I knew I wasn't imagining it. It was my front door knocker, rattling in the middle of the night. I decided to slowly and surely tiptoe downstairs, without making any noise. I suddenly stopped, the silence was deafening. A shadow came from behind me, his hand grabbed my mouth to muffle my screams. I thought I was going to be as dead as a doornail and not make it out alive, but I was so wrong...

AISLING DEVLIN (14)

Cardinal Newman Catholic School, Coventry

THE CREATURE

I walked around the house bored, I tried thinking of things to do, the only idea that came to my mind was to go for a walk. I got into my car and drove to the forest. It was getting dark, at that time I thought the cold air would be refreshing and it was until I saw 'it'. The creature stood forty feet tall towering over me, its flesh looked as if it was rusty metal, sirens nested on its head. As I began to run, I heard the sirens calling out sounding like my mother, my dead mother...

PATRICK MALISZEWSKI (13)
Cardinal Newman Catholic School, Coventry

THE CREEPY SHACK

I was down at the river and it was a super dark night. The stars twinkled and the river was calm. I stumbled across an abandoned shack. I heard a bang that sent shivers up my spine, within this moment I knew my life was in danger. I entered through the half-opened door and once inside I froze. Standing in front of me was a creature I have never seen before. It jumped at me and all I could do was scream an ear-splitting scream. It stopped in front of me and I knew I would die tonight...

KIAN MURRAY (12)
Cardinal Newman Catholic School, Coventry

THE CHASE

As he was running he heard others scream in agony. He quickly turned into the hall, he heard footsteps approaching so he quickly spotted a ladder that looked like it was going to snap if it had any pressure put on it. As the unknown figure turned the corner, Jake knew he had to stop his heavy breathing or he would end it up like the others. As he watched, what seemed like a very tall slim man walked past under him. A drop of sweat dropped and the man stopped and spotted Jake...

DANIIL BANYS (12)
Cardinal Newman Catholic School, Coventry

THE SPOOKS

It was a cold night, some teenagers were on a helicopter ride. They kept hearing some creaky noises at the back of the helicopter but they didn't think too much about it as they were having fun and having conversations. Suddenly, there was a massive bang, an error flashed and the helicopter was on fire over a pitch-black forest. They crashed. They found an abandoned mansion in the forest and two of them went inside. One of the teenagers started to have hallucinations and she disappeared. The other teenager shouted her name until she saw... the monster!

ETHAN MOTTERSHEAD (12)
Denton Community College, Denton

DEATH DOORS

One gruelling night, Mark woke up in a haunted house. Slowly he crept down the stairs, the shadows following him down. Then he heard a noise, he looked back and no one was there. Suddenly, the windows blew open and the walls creased up with veins! Mark went into the kitchen and saw the food that looked twenty years old. He saw the garden that looked more abandoned than the house. He felt a tap on the shoulder. He turned and then he heard a creepy laugh. He walked to the basement and looked inside. Someone screamed and Mark disappeared...

JAMIE ARRANDALE (13)
Denton Community College, Denton

SHADOW MAN CHASE

It was late at night when we arrived at the mansion. We told each other to meet back at the entrance at 3am. Everyone scattered and started on the main floor, I would have too if it wasn't for the dark shadow standing on the hollow staircase. I shivered and followed the distorted shadow to the attic. The door locked behind me and that was the moment I realised this was my fate. The shadow stood in front of me and lashed its bony hands towards my face. Everything went black. Its cackling laugh was the last thing I heard.

JESSICA-FAYTH BRINDLEY (13)
Denton Community College, Denton

JUST A DREAM?

I had been rambling through the forests, only to my delight there was no hotel.
There was only a small cottage on the edge of the lake - I had decided to take
shelter there since it was foggy and misty. As I entered I heard the creaking of
the floorboards against my feet...
"Hello?" I asked. No reply. "Hello?" I repeated. A little louder. I then walked outside - to find the owner. I then got distracted by the gushing of the sky-blue waves reflecting on the sunrise. I had strolled closer...
Bang! It was a dream. I then saw her...

ZARA ALI

Elizabeth Garrett Anderson Language College For Girls, London

COUNTESS CONSTANZA

The foggy mist hovered over the dark, cold river as Countess Constanza walked along the bridge. Hatton Garden wasn't too far now, but the coldness took to her bones, such that it slowed her pace. As she was making her way, the infamous scoundrel Jack tripped over her expensive gown, causing them to plummet to a heap.
"Sorry, Miss!" he muttered.
The revellers spilled from The Castle Pub and they noticed blood.
"Ere! It's the Countess!" one shouted.
She was found on Hatton Garden, dismembered... Yet her heart was still pumping blood...

KEIRA JOHNSON
Elizabeth Garrett Anderson Language College For Girls, London

SPINE-CHILLER

My palms began to sweat as I twisted the door knob. Pitch-black. The door slammed shut. "Hello?" I quivered, my voice trembling with fright. As I looked around, squinting my eyes, I saw coffins. My nose shrivelled with disgust. The stench was unbearable. The candle in my hand began to flicker. I heard faint footsteps behind me. My legs began to shake uncontrollably and tears of fear streamed down my face. I felt ice-cold fingertips trace down my neck. I screamed as a hand covered my mouth, making it hard to breathe. Suddenly, tranquillity walked in....

HANNIFAH KHANOM (13)

Elizabeth Garrett Anderson Language College For Girls, London

THE BASEMENT

I walked in shaking. It was cold, dark, damp and dusty. The smell was foul, it was so foul I felt like I was going to vomit. The pungent odour got worse and I stepped closer to the basement door. It felt like the whole entire world was waiting for this moment, this moment that would reveal the truth about Sir Renegade's death. I tiptoed across the floor to the basement door. With my candle in my hand, I opened the door to reveal... *whoosh!* The candle blew out. I never saw light again...

ESME JORDAN (12)
Epsom College, Epsom

OFF-LIMITS

"Stop, Jess! You know it's off-limits," exclaimed Charlie with fear in her eyes.

"I know," Jess replied but she had already begun edging down the cold stone steps which led to darkness. Above her, bottle-green windows rattled menacingly as the wind howled against them. Her hands were trembling as she slid the tight lock open which protected the secret she was about to unfold. Towering shadows were cast around her, her heart paced as footsteps surrounded her. A gloom-filled mist crawled along the deserted corridor as a sharp nail wrapped around her chestnut curls and pulled her down...

HANNAH FOY (13)

Highcliffe School, Highcliffe

TOBY

Toby wasn't picking up her calls, her texts left unanswered. For weeks, nothing. Into the forest, Toby disappeared. Devoured by eternal fog, Shela was devastated. Lost in never-ending sorrow, the dark forest around was all that was left. A scraping sound broke the isolation, Shela looked up: 'You weren't there for me, it was your fault Shela' was carved into a neighbouring tree. The fog suddenly rolled in, blocking the moonlight. Darkness, back where she began. *Snap!* Shela turned. "Toby." Cracked, ancient hands reached out for her. "Toby? You're not Toby..."

JACK DAVIS (13)
Highcliffe School, Highcliffe

THE HOUSE OF HORROR

Fog crashed into crumbling walls of an abandoned house that Chloe and Matthew were the first to explore. Darkness consumed the hallways and Chloe trembled, due to both coldness and fear, especially when Matthew didn't answer her calls! A loud bang urged Chloe towards it but when she arrived, she saw nothing but some paper... 'I have Matthew, come find me if you want him to live!' it read. Terrified, she followed the footsteps that echoed through the building until she reached an ominous forest outside. She followed the crunch of leaves until it fell silent. Then everything went black...

SOPHIE DONALDSON (13)

Highcliffe School, Highcliffe

If You Go Down To The Woods Today...

They crept out of the house at midnight, into the woods. It was dark, the wind whistled and owls were hooting. They spotted an abandoned cottage, Amy and Jasmine held onto each other as they went to explore, hoping to feel safer than they did out in the woods. As they walked into the cottage, bats started circling their heads and a wolf howled in the distance. The gale made the windows and doors rattle. The front door slammed behind them. Footsteps sounded like someone or something was getting closer. The girls were shaking. "Hello," they said quietly...

Harriet Jones (12)
Highcliffe School, Highcliffe

UNTITLED

Tom slid under the rusted gate, the house leaned over him. Windows were boarded and fog was seeping through small holes in the walls. He kicked the rotten door off its hinges and reluctantly stepped in. Cockroaches were scattering away into the vast, empty rooms ahead. The floorboards creaked as he made his way through the doorway. A sense of foreboding struck him, he saw a shadow in the corner - half-lit by the moonlight. Tom tried to run but he couldn't. Why, why couldn't he move? The shadow moved towards him, he felt an icy hand on his arm...

HARRISON PARKER (12)

Highcliffe School, Highcliffe

SHE HAD TO GO

She turned around slowly taking in her worrying surroundings and wondering how she got there. As she came to a stop, voices started to surround her, whispering in her ear, making her tingle and not in a good way! Holding her head, she started screaming, trying to drown the voices out. It didn't work, they got louder and louder. She looked towards the mouldy church door and saw a person reaching out to save her. Stumbling, she ran towards the door and went inside.

The next day, her body was found ripped to shreds. The DNA was from a wolf!

AMELIA LARYEA (13)

Highcliffe School, Highcliffe

THE FIGURE

It went black, Josh screamed. "Mum!" he cried in despair. He waited for a while but there was no reply. "Mum!" he cried again. "Where are you?" As he waited for a reply again, Josh started to panic. He tried the light switches but none of them were turning on. There was a crash from upstairs and Josh flew up. "Is that you, Mum?" he yelled. There was a bang from downstairs and Josh leapt down there, taking the steps two at a time. The light in the kitchen flicked on and a black silhouette stood there...

TOBY STADDON (13)
Highcliffe School, Highcliffe

THE DIARY

Jack was exploring the twisted forest when it started hailing. The trees provided little shelter so Jack headed for an old decrepit hut on the distant hill. Once inside, he found a tattered diary. Jack started to read, the diary seemed normal at first but soon took a sinister turn, the writing ended halfway through a word. A thunderclap resounded in the forest then a whisper came from behind him which said, "Go to sleep, child." The sound of a chainsaw filled the air, followed by a terrifying scream and then all was silent.

TAYLA HEWITT (12)
Highcliffe School, Highcliffe

WENDIGO

With great luck I tumbled through the half-open window, although I hit my now bloodied hand on the frame. Trying not to notice the pain, I slammed the window shut. Seconds later it froze, leaving an array of beautiful patterns on the glass. Looking back I saw it had caught up to me! I entered the living room of the lodge and darted to the front door, locking it shut. I sat down, all was silent but momentarily broken by heavy breathing. Two deep black eyes fell into my lap. The things from the nightmares were right behind me...

MOSES HARRY (13)
Highcliffe School, Highcliffe

MIDNIGHT DASH

Raven sprinted through the forest, trees grabbed at her shoulders and the rain drenched her clothes. "Jessica!" she screamed into the darkness. "Where are you, Jessica?" She reached a clearing in the woods, she stopped abruptly with tears streaming down her muddy face. "Je- "
Her yell was interrupted by an eerie whisper, "Jessica won't be coming back!"
Before Raven could escape, a hand clenched onto her shoulder and she felt herself begin to fall down, down, down...

SCARLETT ADAMS (13)
Highcliffe School, Highcliffe

THE STRANGER

Ashley was driving home when he suddenly realised he didn't have enough petrol to get him there. He was driving past a castle so he went in and sat down. He called his brother to pick him up in five minutes. Ten minutes went by and he still wasn't there. *Bang!* A wall fell down and Ashley stared at the moon in fear. He felt the wind pick up. *Bang!* Lightning struck the grass and made a fire. As he was sitting there in fear, he felt a hand touch him on his back. Ashely turned around...

BEN ALDRED (14)
Highcliffe School, Highcliffe

THE WORLD STARTS OVER

3... 2... 1... The school bell rings, marking the weekend. I run out of school, down North Lane. It's a cold and grey day and I see Mr Tapping, my neighbour, trying to cut down his oak tree. He claims to be good at gardening but keeps missing. It's almost like the tree is dodging his blade. I smile and move on to my house. Dad is acting strange so I do my homework and get ready for bed...

If only I knew what was about to happen that night I would have tried to escape, escape on a ship...

BEL BARTLETT (13)

Highcliffe School, Highcliffe

Trapped

Heavy breathing fills the atmosphere, I can barely move in this 'suit'. Something large and porcelain creeps past me, barely dodging my suit. I try to lift my head, hoping to find a lock but I'm stopped by something piercing my arm. I'm trapped. I watch as the figure walks past again, more aware. I can hear the thudding of its feet on the marble floor. Everything goes silent, I shut my eyes for a few seconds. When I open them, bright eyes are staring back at me, our eyes locking...

Millie Musker (12)

Highcliffe School, Highcliffe

HER

We've been together for seven years. She's 5 ft 2 and has long blonde hair. We've done so much together: our first apartment, our first dog. She has such a nice personality and a brilliant sense of humour. I love her so much, so much. We'll get married one day and it will be spectacular. I know the way she walks up the stairs, we've been together for seven years. I'm glad she knows it now. She's in the basement. It's time. She's mine!

HARPER SCOTFORD (13)

Highcliffe School, Highcliffe

Rebirth

Light seeped through, I tried to grab the light, it was flowing through my fingertips. My house was now desolate, no finger had been placed on anything in my bedroom. Moonlight crept through the open windows when I heard a loud creak. I turned around, the door was wide open and a shadow lurked behind. *I must be tired,* I thought. *I must be dreaming!* I closed the window and turned around, goosebumps creeping up my neck and then it grabbed me...

Jessica Hefferan (13)

Highcliffe School, Highcliffe

THE HOUSE OF THE SHADOWS

I opened the door to the old, abandoned house that sat high on a hill and instantly felt I was not alone. I had been dared to spend the night. The wind whistled through the cracks in the boarded-up windows and the shadows reflected off the moonlight and moved as if they had one job: to close in on me. A door creaked open ahead, a sound that echoed off the walls. I felt an ice-cold hand on my shoulder and as I took a breath, I realised it could be my last...

LOGAN SMITH (13)

Highcliffe School, Highcliffe

SCHOOL

The Queen's Academy for Creative Minds closed in 1876. Bob and Phil entered the desolate building, layers of dust filled the old corridor. From the moment that they had stepped in, the storm outside had worsened. They saw the door to Class 5, many had gone mad there so logically... they went inside! *Creak!* The floorboards shook as they walked. Suddenly they heard it... "You're late!" Afterwards, everything went dark.

JONAH SARGENT (12)
Highcliffe School, Highcliffe

WHERE ARE YOU?

My wellington boots squelched in the mud. Rain splattered down my teary face, I was looking for my friend Aubrey. "Aubrey!" I called thousands of times, but there was no answer. The trees towered over me. My heart burst, her body lay on the ground, ripped apart; organs torn. Who could have done this? What could have done this? Out of the bushes appeared a deformed woman, her limbs crooked, her eyes beaming with scarlet red. Blood dripped from her fangs. My breathing was even sharper. Lightning struck, she was gone! I then felt hot, rancid breath on the back of my neck...

ZARA LATIF (12)
Kensington Park School, London

SPINE-CHILLER

An October night has always been an indisputably cold event, but when at sea and when the tide comes back to the lands, it brings things that have fallen to its strength and guile back to the sands. The bodies which had drifted that demonic night rendered a truly horrific sight, as the moon lit up their rubbery, cold faces and blood lingered with the rotting wood, lifelessly drifting among the wet rocks. A body of water cannot be without depth and with depth comes darkness and terror - things that lurk in the shadows, things that eat, things that kill...

HENRY THORNTON (12)
Kensington Park School, London

THE CUP

The night was freezing, suddenly a sound that was more like a gunshot was heard. The police came to where they thought the sound came from. A horrific murder had happened right in the middle of a dark forest and the full moon was the only witness. Whilst investigating the death of the local art teacher, an old detective found a cup and uncovered a legend about a supernaturally-cursed cup. He remembered it instantly, his grandma told him about it every night. As soon as someone used the cup, the person had 150 days left to live...

MARILENA BORS (12)
Kensington Park School, London

COMING TO ME

I barely had any sleep last night. All I remember was the sound of a key turning and a lock clicking shut. The wallpaper was ripped and only just hanging on. The wood on the small chest of drawers was rotten, much the same as everything else. From downstairs I could hear voices, voices I did not know. I opened the wooden framed door covered in a thick red something or other. The lock clicked open, I pushed the door open and ran across the creaky floorboards. I could hear the people from downstairs coming, coming for me...

MILLIE MCDONALD (12)
Kensington Park School, London

She's Gone

I just stood there, silent, my mouth hung open. She lay there cold, pale and still, there was no life left in her. Her dark hair swept across her face, her brown eyes glassy and stared into nothing. A shadow towered over the small patch she lay in, I shivered, my mouth still gaping at the sight before me. I stood there for a while, every now and then some parakeets flew over us and it reminded me of the freedom she once had. This was it, there was nothing I could do, she was gone...

Kitty Kinsman (12)
Kensington Park School, London

DANCE WITH DEIMOS

Cold. Despair. Gloom. Then, murderous mirth indefatigably crawling over my shell. Picking up my pace, the ichor escaping my pulsating limb. Like a great monsoon, tears chasing down my sullen face. Sinister sound singing again. Drums of darkness crashing upon my fragile mind. Hope, fluttering away from me, crying its crocodile tears: Helping Ixtab's aim. Reduced to an animal, my plodding slowed. Like a plague, fear seized me. Blood now ice. Horrid hysterics scuttled at my eardrums. It was here... Screaming. Pain. Suffering. The unearthly force savagely tearing. Chest rupturing. Pain slithers down my spine. I'm praying for death.

THOMAS WHENTRINGHAME (16)

Maidstone Grammar School, Maidstone

EQUIVOCATIONS OF THE NIGHT

The pain was surreal, thick ichor dripped from my stump of a wrist. I slumped against a splintered, wooden door. My silence kept me alive, fighting the will to scream. Tears danced maliciously down my cheeks, teasing me as they jumped from my chin, joining the blood on the floor. An involuntary whimper escaped my lips. Knowing what I'd done; trepidation filled my soul. The floorboards creaked... A sour, sulphurous scent advanced into my nostrils. My body became a statue, each heartbeat thrashed violently against my ribcage. Slowly, I turned. My gaze finding a single, glowing eye. Shaking, I sighed...

JACK WHENTRINGHAME (16)

Maidstone Grammar School, Maidstone

DO NOT ENTER THE WOODS

Billy was the new boy in a creepy neighbourhood. Nobody spoke to him or to each other. They shuffled around in sinister silence. The only information given was 'never go into the woods'.

Inquisitive, he crept out in the dead of night, nervously stumbling through the murky darkness towards the daunting tangle of trees. Something inside him dared him to enter. The wooded canopy loomed over as if staring down at the unusual creature below. The further he went, the more he felt consumed.

The ground started to move beneath his feet, the trees began a demonic shaking... Billy vanished.

OLIVER LA TORRE
Newland House School, Twickenham

NO ONE CAN HEAR YOU SCREAM

You're so engrossed exploring outside the derelict Gothic mansion, that you pay no attention to the weather. First you know of the storm is rain pelting down on you. You don't mean to trespass but it's an emergency. Your hair won't survive. There's shelter in the mansion and the door's ajar. Lightning slashes the sky as you slip into the hall.
Your eyes take a moment to adjust to the murky light. But you sense evil before you see the remains. A fellow goth, judging from the accessories surrounding the bones. A creature cackles. Thunder drowns out your screams...

BEN HARRIS
Newland House School, Twickenham

THE MIDDLE CRATE

Rain pounded the ground and the wind whirled past me as I approached the old bungalow. I opened the wooden door, stepped inside and saw a derelict, old room. "Go inside..." the voice inside my head said. But why? It spoke again, telling me to enter another room, similar, but with three large, metallic crates at the side. Opening one, I found a stack of books, useless to me. "Open the middle crate," the voice commanded me. Inside, I was shocked to find another box containing photos, cards and other artefacts from my childhood, in this very house!

BLAKE HADEN (13)
Newland House School, Twickenham

STILL AS A STATUE

Rain pelted the ground, unforgiving and relentless. Low clouds rumbled over the street, bringing with them a desperate gloom. The twins looked at their new home, enjoying every aspect of its grandeur.

The girls set about exploring the house. Hinges squealed in protest as Madge pushed a door. At the foot of a broken bed stood a cupboard.

A blood-curdling scream filled the air. Without thinking, the neighbour's boy rushed to the sound. Smashing the lock on a window, he clambered into a dark room. There stood two young girls, still as statues. Turned to stone.

MILES BELL (13)

Newland House School, Twickenham

Rag Doll

Wrapped in the comfort of my woollen blanket, I dozed in bed. An ear-splitting shriek burst from the forest which soon turned into sobs. Anxiously, I ambled towards the window that overlooked the haunting forest. I could see her wailing by solemn trees, clutching what looked to be a rag doll. Out of nowhere, her head slowly tilted towards me, making chilling eye contact. My heart pounding, I yanked the curtains together.

The next morning, I saw my mother lying lifeless on the floor. Horrified, I turned to her bed to see the same rag doll smiling at me.

Tim Wright (13)
Newland House School, Twickenham

THE BECKONING DOOR

Like a burglar tiptoeing silently, I crept along the hallway - shadows watching. Where was I? Why was I here? All I remembered was my name: Thomas, and that this wasn't a place I wanted to be. Colossal arches loomed over me and the quietness disturbed me. At the end of the hallway, a door, beckoning to be opened. Thunder suddenly crashed down on the roof. Slowly I began my approach. Ten metres. Five metres. Two metres. And then I was right by it. Cautiously, I twisted the decaying handle and the door slowly creaked open. Then I saw it...

DIMITRI TZINIERIS
Newland House School, Twickenham

The Grandma

Gradually, I rose from my rock-hard bed and paced around the shadowy room. The notes on the wall from previous victims gave instructions to find a key to the front door to flee my dungeon. Yet that key was inside a safe, which required a code hidden somewhere in the labyrinth-like, ancient house. Carefully, I trod down the creaky hallway. Then I saw her. The wretched creature that trapped me in my cell. I had to avoid her deathly gaze at all costs. But, like an owl, her head swivelled round to look directly at me. Death was now inevitable.

James G-S

Newland House School, Twickenham

A FULL MOON

Cautiously I clambered over the wall, strangled by ivy. The ground felt sodden from the pouring rain. A deathly silence engulfed me. As I looked up, I saw it. Shining in the sky was the full moon. It only meant one thing. Werewolves. Suddenly a silhouetted figure on the horizon howled into the night. Did werewolves hunt in packs? I didn't know but I knew that they would not spare me. I ran. But not fast enough as they swiftly tracked me down. I was surrounded. They had stalked me like a hawk seeking its prey. My outlook was bleak.

EDWARD KNOTT
Newland House School, Twickenham

Screaming Wind

Wind was lashing against the windows and hammering at the glass. It screamed over the house and beat a fist against the roof. Opening the heavy creaky door, I entered. The eerie silence and the smell of pain and death worried me. Walking up the ancient wooden stairs, I heard something. Frantically, I sprinted and hid behind the door of an empty room. Someone was with me. Were they following me? I sneezed from the dust in the air around me. Should I run or stay behind the door? I hoped and prayed they didn't come to find me...

Dylan Grewal (12)
Newland House School, Twickenham

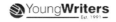

HIM AND THE THING

It was a sunny day. He was playing outside with his friends when a man in a clown costume suddenly appeared in a big bush. The thing coaxed him over so he left his friends and wandered over. He turned around and his friends instantly vanished. The thing and him teleported to a dark, creepy house, where the thing forced him to watch his friends and family be horrifically tortured. He desperately tried to stop the thing and held his breath as his mum was brutally murdered. Out of nowhere he started maniacally laughing. He was the thing all along!

TASIAN THOMAS (11)
Nightingale Community Academy, Tooting

THE NUN

Who's there? I wondered. I heard an ominous creak. "I have to get out of this place, she's coming for me!" I couldn't let her have it. She would kill anyone who got in her way. She was after a sacred book that I got from a charity shop. If she failed to find it she would have to answer to some dangerous criminals. She had followed me to an abandoned house, but I managed to escape through the back streets... The next day, the police discovered a body riddled with bullet holes and dressed in a nun's habit.

JAYLEN SOUTH (12)
Nightingale Community Academy, Tooting

THE BOY

One stormy night, in an alley, there was a scary boy wearing all black. He was an alien in disguise and his monstrous friend lived in the sewer. As a man was walking past, he dropped his phone and saw the monster. It snatched and dragged him down to the sewer.

The next day, the man was on the news having disappeared. They warned people to stay inside. The scary boy went outside, killing people left to right.

In the morning, the monster died when the sun penetrated the sewer and the boy changed his appearance to slime and escaped.

YAHYA KAMAL (11)

Nightingale Community Academy, Tooting

THE RED EYES

"They'll never find me!" I was in a lab, sprinting away from them. It smelt like gas and the lab was huge. The floor was hard and slippery. I could see lots of coloured potions. As the robots entered, they glowed red and had automatic machine guns. The robots tried to kill me as I stole an energy bean that made robots bigger. I ran out of my lab and to my car. I drove away at the speed of light. Just as I thought I had lost them, one jumped out of my back seat. Those red eyes...

BRANDON PAGE (12)
Nightingale Community Academy, Tooting

My Stolen Breath

I knew I wouldn't make it back and just before I knew it the church bells chimed. My legs stopped running and my body dropped to the floor. I felt restricted. I couldn't move or breathe. As if someone was holding me down. But no one was there. "Help me!" I screamed. "Someone, please." No response was to be heard. Out of nowhere, people started to appear but not ordinary people, they had white gowns on and animal masks covering their faces. Slowly they started to hold hands and spin around in a circle singing, "Ring-a-ring-o'-roses..."

CHLOE PERVERSI (15)
Radnor House Sevenoaks School, Sundridge

THE DREAD OF DEATH

The silence was deadly, Darla knew that death wasn't far behind. She ran as fast as her shaky legs could take her, not even daring to peer over her shoulder. Suddenly, before Darla had time to avoid it, she tripped over an upturned carpet and smashed her head against the grand piano. Darla arose, head buzzing, blood gushing from her disfigured forehead. "I must have blacked out," Darla said, as her watch now read 3:34am. Darla just sat there in shock and panic. The thirteen-year-old felt something wet dripping onto her palms and realised her wrists were slit...

JAMES HORI (13)

Radnor House Sevenoaks School, Sundridge

Her Last Breath

"Are we playing hide-and-seek? Well, I'm very good at this game. Come, come out wherever you are. I know you are here," its voice whispered. Emma held her breath, she crawled from under the bed and stood to try and run out of the room. No escape. The man wearing a black mask stopped her. "Help! Help me!" cried Emma.
A sudden silence, a silence so long but not long enough. There was a loud gunshot but everything fell silent. Emma dropped dead on the floor, her last breath left, along with her life. Tired eyes close, her heart softened...

Tilly Beckerman (12)
Radnor House Sevenoaks School, Sundridge

Around The Corner

There were two boys, Will and Max, who went exploring in the woods. As they were walking, Will slipped and fell into a dark cave! Max heard a scream from Will, so he jumped down to help him. Will, Max's little brother, was hurt and scared, they were stuck, trapped underground. The only way out was through this mysterious tunnel. They started to walk. Will was clinging on to Max's arm. They heard a creak... Max told Will to stay there while he went to explore. Minutes passed, then hours, Will called. There was no response... This was the end...

Charlie Paye (13)

Radnor House Sevenoaks School, Sundridge

MY LAST VISITOR

Her eyes awoke with misery. He was there looking at her. Lightning struck, a loud terrible scream cracked one of her mum's picture frames. Unfortunately, her mum passed away a few years ago and the picture was the only memory of her mum. She moved to the picture... He pulled out a shiny knife and her eyes burst out of her brain. He walked closer and whispered, "Home alone, no one to save you!" He raised the sharp knife and sliced it straight through her heart. A sudden explosion of blood hit him; his grim smile painted a grim red.

IONA DAY (13)

Radnor House Sevenoaks School, Sundridge

CAMPING

It was 3am, the wind was howling. I was camping with Dad in the Black Forest. I hated my camping trips with my dad, something bad happened every time. When I woke up there was the cracking of branches all around the tent and a silent whisper which sounded like, "Blood, we crave blood, blood, blood. Get out of our woods, it's ours! Leave!" I shook my dad, but he didn't wake up. I rolled him towards me and to my horror, his eyes were completely missing, they were just black holes. Suddenly, the tent's zip undone itself...

MAX HARRISON (13)
Radnor House Sevenoaks School, Sundridge

Blair

The little girl slept peacefully in the sight of danger. A man as thin as a stick stiffly turned the doorknob on the other side. The tiny girl tossed and turned in her four-poster bed that was placed directly in front of the old door she had. This little girl named Blair loved bleak happenings which often creeped and confused the people of her town - stabbings. Her personality was very black, smug. Blair opened her hazel eyes and looked up... Blood fell from her face and body, cuts and bruises draped across Blair. She smiled with relief.

Matilda Simons (11)
Radnor House Sevenoaks School, Sundridge

NO RELIEF

Sharp and cold, the sensation of death as I felt the nerves move down my back. The weapon, not quite slicing the skin but hard enough to make a mark. The movement was circling around the body, waiting to strike. It was like my heart was going to fall out my chest. Then it happened. A hideous pain starting from the top of the neck to the bottom of the back. Crimson blood stained the room around me. The body squirming for relief. *Poor girl,* I thought, *she should have known she would end up alone, end up underground.*

ISOBEL KING (14)
Radnor House Sevenoaks School, Sundridge

THE CRACK

He screamed, it attacked. She panicked. The monster grabbed him and dragged him to the shallows. She leapt on the bed and shrieked. She waited and then it was back. It peeked round the door and scratched the wood. He crushed the walls of the room into her. The space got smaller and smaller, the creature stalked her as she pushed the walls but it was no use, the monster vanished. She darted to the door and struggled to breathe as the walls kept compressing. She barely managed to move on her side. The door was right there, not yet...

EDWARD SHILLING (14)

Radnor House Sevenoaks School, Sundridge

THE TRAP

The wind was swirling, the bells were ringing, everything was wet from the terrible storm that had hit. Iona was in the middle of the woods, soaking wet. She didn't know how she got there but she had been there for a while. Iona stood up and started to walk, suddenly she found an old, broken garage in the middle of nowhere. She walked inside, the floor creaked and then she saw a door but the door was locked. *Bang!* The door had been locked; it was a trap. Someone was trying to kill her. There was no way out...

CHARLOTTE FLENGHI (13)
Radnor House Sevenoaks School, Sundridge

THE AXE

There were two people in a decrepit haunted house. One normal, one not. One man armed himself with a sharpened axe made to kill. It was like a game for him. The weapon shimmering in the darkness, ready to take the life of his next victim. She was sleeping soundly while the predator got closer! There was one door between them. He was rising his weapon, ready to swing... First he chopped her, by this time she was screaming in agony but he didn't care. First a finger, next the head and she wasn't his last victim...

JOSH HASSAN (12)

Radnor House Sevenoaks School, Sundridge

A Star In A Black Sea

All's safe now that she's dead they say but what about me, her best friend and the one who killed her? Wherever I turn she's there holding the knife, dripping with her rosy blood. They say I'm safe, they say I'm just a bit ill from the sudden change but really they are covering up that I loved her and now I am ill from the trauma of her death that I caused. I could have saved her by being her girlfriend but no, I am as deadly as she was in her last minutes. I hear her words echoing...

Alice Munn (11)

Radnor House Sevenoaks School, Sundridge

THE SHADOW

I woke up shivering, the covers had been ripped off. The sign of chaos sent a shiver down my spine. I was so tired that I had slept through all of this! I got up, only to be greeted by a gust of glacial wind. I tiptoed towards the door. The monster must have heard the creak from the door. I stopped dead in my tracks, something was watching me through the mirror at the back of the corridor. But how? A hand had been placed on my shoulder. I hesitated but ended up turning around, my last regret...

WILL SMITH (13)

Radnor House Sevenoaks School, Sundridge

ARGH!

On a blacked-out, gloomy night in November, two families arrived in Edinburgh looking forward to their trip. Rain was pouring down, washing the thick blanket of moss from the windows. Something wasn't right as they stepped into the house for the first time, they were intrigued. Door after door after corridor, it seemed the house was a never-ending, mysterious maze. The youngest found a secret room. Suddenly they heard a door slam, followed by a piercing scream from upstairs. Then the lights went out and it was pitch-black... "Argh!" They were never heard of or seen again!

LEWIS MERRYWEATHER (13)
Sir Robert Pattinson Academy, North Hykeham

THE TREACHEROUS TIME

As I was strolling through the forest, walking my dog, I muttered, "Ugh, it's going to rain." Suddenly, small drops landed on my nose and hair. Then lightning flashed and something growled in the bushes, my dog tensed and growled at where the noise was coming from. Suddenly, a huge black creature pounced at me, it had human hands and feet yet the rest of it was wolfish. "A werewolf!" I stammered as it bit my dog in half. Suddenly it scratched me. Hair appeared on my arms and legs and a long snout grew on my hairy, scratched face...

MATTHEW ROWE (11)

Sir Robert Pattinson Academy, North Hykeham

THE SHADOW

The mist hovered over the ground; fog protruded from my mouth as I walked through the forest with my torch illuminating the path before me. I couldn't help but feel the hard stare of someone behind me, or something! I was completely alone in the forest, so I thought! *Snap!* A discreet sound came from the direction in which I felt the stare earlier. I turned around and saw nothing. As I turned back around, I picked up the pace, every stride covering the ground. Then I stopped dead in my tacks and hesitantly turned around to see a shadow...

LEWIS KIRK (12)

Sir Robert Pattinson Academy, North Hykeham

THE HOUSE

The house in the woods was unusual, everything about it was scary. The bricks were charcoal-grey and the windows were smashed. Inside the house, carpets and walls were stained red and the scent of blood was too much. Anyone who stepped into the house was dead in five seconds. People recalled seeing a face pop up in the window every time they walked past. The house was packed with dolls and statues. The furniture was upside down, each floorboard creaked and each light flickered on and off. One day, a boy entered and he was dead seconds later...

ROSIE WILKINS (12)

Sir Robert Pattinson Academy, North Hykeham

THE MISTAKE

I opened my eyes when I shouldn't have, the dumb mistake I made led to misery. It led to darkness and it was cold and dreary. I couldn't really make out the picture, but what I could make out in the diminutive beam of light was a single chair stood there silently. It felt like I was chained to the floor. Was anything restricting me? It was very strange. What was happening? The chair was still there, isolated. It looked lonely and sad, I didn't know how. I was stuck and there was another puzzling thing, someone was coming...

ISABELLA KERRISON (12)
Sir Robert Pattinson Academy, North Hykeham

THE BLACK LAKE

A sense of dread radiated from the lake, lurking in the darkness out of sight, slowly getting closer as the bright moon slowly crept beyond the horizon. My heart raced as fear crept upon me, taking hold of my rationality like a snake slowly suffocating its prey. I inched towards the black lake, its infinite waters calling on my soul like a fish being reeled in on a hook. I touched the icy waters, the cold relieved me, relaxing my muscles. A slender hand as white as snow slid out of the opaque liquid, clasping hold of my scrawny leg...

LOGAN EDWARD WAKEFIELD (13)

Sir Robert Pattinson Academy, North Hykeham

THE NOISE

It was 9.30pm and my friends dared me to go into the abandoned mansion - so stupidly, I did! Inside, I saw things no thirteen-year-old should ever see! Spiders the size of a baby's fist crawled the floor in a stealthy manner but the thing that creeped me out the most was a sound, it was somewhat like a strange clicking noise. When I reached the door the sound was coming from, I opened it with a creak... Right in front of me was a child's doll! It turned its head at me and started walking in my direction...

PHOEBE HARDIE (11)
Sir Robert Pattinson Academy, North Hykeham

DARKEST DEPTHS

Darkness was all around me, circling like vultures. It was sucking all the life and colour out of me like a vacuum, conflicted of my whereabouts? I crept into the darkness until I found a little girl crying. I tapped her shoulder and she suddenly stopped crying and began laughing. She turned her head, her face was replaced with pure darkness! I fell backwards and couldn't stop falling. I curled up into a ball, expecting to hit the ground hard. Suddenly I woke up so it was just a dream! I hoped anyway...

THOMAS DICKINSON (12)
Sir Robert Pattinson Academy, North Hykeham

BREATH

My eyes opened, silence, I was alone. I rose from my bed and my battalion uniform crumpled and cracked as if it had been stuck in the mud for a lifetime. The gunfire had ceased and no one was to be seen. I wandered around searching for any life, it must have been hours - the moon stayed in the centre of all the stars, not moving an inch. Fog seeped onto the ground and the pressure burst my ears to a bleeding pulp. I began sinking, the mud engulfed me like a midnight snack. My last breath escaped.

CALLUM FIELDS (13)
Sir Robert Pattinson Academy, North Hykeham

RUN

The floorboards creak and groan under her weight that they were not designed to bear. Dust swirls in the air like someone is walking towards her. She stands like they all do, her eyes taking in the peeling grey paint and cracking floorboards. Not long now until he comes. He always comes. The girl is moving again, she is walking over to the window. She leans on the frame. *Crack!* She whirls around. I can hear her breathing ragged, sharp. The dust is scattered into a frenzied dance, she starts to relax... Big mistake! He's coming little girl. Run...

REBECCA BALL

Smestow School, Castlecroft

ACADEMY HORROR STORY

There once was a glamorous academy with loads of pure students going there.

It seemed normal but it had a dark side. One night, an athlete came back to collect something but then the academy was different and not in a nice way. The athlete felt like he was being watched... When he collected his item, he was just about to leave when he heard a terrorising sound like a vicious howling wolf. He turned around and saw a wolf...

The next day, everyone was wondering where the athlete was as no one had seen him yet...

GEORGIE HOOPER (11)

Smestow School, Castlecroft

THE BEAST WITHIN

I walk up the path and knock on the door, rain hammering down around me, lightning streaking through the sky. It creaks open. He stalks out of the shadows with his crazed grin. He laughs maniacally, I do too. That is until I see the brown fur on my arms. When I feel the craze for the hunt, I howl. I am running through the graveyard, brambles reaching out for me. I stare up at the moon and howl. His rifle is pointed straight at me. I hear an ear-piercing shriek as my brother sends a bullet through my head.

EVE STAIRMAND-JACKSON
Smestow School, Castlecroft

THE CHEAP HAUNTED HOUSE

It was Saturday, me and my wife were packing our stuff to move into the new house that we just bought. It was contemptible so we didn't wait to buy it, but something bad was waiting for us. Everything was ready and we moved to the new house. We went to sleep but at midnight we heard some noises upstairs, I went to check but I found nothing. When I went back I found my wife dead on the floor. I got scared and felt like someone was watching me. I drove away and never went back to the house.

JASLEEN KAUR (13)
Smestow School, Castlecroft

THE HOUSE ON THE DARK SIDE OF TOWN

It lures you in and won't let you out. Once the tough reedy grass has a clutch of your bare ankles there's no escape and what lives within is far more dangerous than the house itself. The crooked, rotting windows look like eyes, always watching, trying to find their next victim. The enormous, brown door always ajar like the mouth of a tiger open, ready to pounce and seize its prey at any moment. If you fall or tumble outside of this house there shall be no mercy spared. That's the last time you will see the light of day.

OLIVIA GOODWIN (12)

St David's College, Llandudno

THE SMILING MAN

'Twas midnight and a thunderstorm rocked the woods. Jessy was running back to the car after her walk when suddenly she heard footsteps dashing after her. Terrified, she ran even faster, trying not to trip. As soon as Jessy got back to the car, she got in, slammed the car door shut and locked it. There were a few seconds silence and then, *blam!* Screaming, she put her foot down and sped away. Whilst doing this, she looked in the wing mirror and saw a man... a smiling man...

JACOB WILKINSON (11)
St David's College, Llandudno

THE BROKEN TOY

It is a cold night in my old farmhouse in the UK. My name is Jack Mason. It's kind of creepy and I'm pretty sure I can hear giggles in the vents, but no one believes me, except my little brother, Mikey. He thinks he can hear it too. It reminds me of a toy I used to have. It has a stitched mouth and an eye missing. *What is that?* I think. I just heard a creak. I grab my foam baseball bat. I hear it again... *Creeeaaak!* It's coming closer...

JACK KENNEDY (12)

St David's College, Llandudno

Shadows In The Moonlight

The fog started crawling in. "I'll never be back before dark," I said. Thunder and lightning escaped from the clouds, outlining weather-beaten tombs and gravestones around me. A mysterious, ancient building came into view. "I'll wait in there and call Jack, he will come and get me." I sneaked between the ancient monuments and reached the door; the latch was decaying but was unlocked. I entered, the door slamming behind me. "Hello?" Silence. Trembling, I called Jack. He was thirty minutes away. Great! Moonlight cast dancing figures on the stained glass windows, a cold touch breezed past my arm. "Jack...?"

Rebecca Sales (12)

St John's Catholic Comprehensive School, Gravesend

FOR THE LOVE OF SCIENCE

I don't get it, why were they screaming? All shouting at the top of their voices, shrieking like wild animals, it doesn't make any sense whatsoever. What I was doing wasn't even that painful so their whining had no purpose. Don't they know they are contributing to science? Shouldn't that give them peace of mind? They signed up to do this. I may not have told them what they were signing up for, but that still doesn't warrant all this palaver. But at least that's out of the way. Now it's time to attach all the body parts!

EMEKA ESENWA (14)
St John's Catholic Comprehensive School, Gravesend

THE EXHAUSTING CRY

The place was isolated. The police presumed it was abduction; pushing to know more. Her helpless parents with their endless love were fighting to find their child. Almost too hard! Did they want the pity for losing the child that they never really knew? Every frosty night, if you were really quiet, you could hear the wretched and desperate cry as though she was still there perhaps, or just in their hearts. I should know for I am that child. Screaming by night, searching by day for love. The agony of being trapped down here is pure torture!

STEPHANIE KINGSLAND (12)
St John's Catholic Comprehensive School, Gravesend

A Frightening Night

I came home from school to find myself alone in the house. My parents were at work and I had approximately an hour before they got home. It was at this time that I started to notice things were missing: the computer, the TV, our family photographs. I waited and waited for my parents to come home, the time when they should have arrived came and went so I was worried. That's when I noticed how quiet it was. Everywhere there was silence. Where was everyone? The cars? The people coming home from work? The birds? Am I truly alone?

BIANKA LATKA (12)

St John's Catholic Comprehensive School, Gravesend

THE ABANDONED ASYLUM

The phone rang. "Hello?"

"Help me!"

"Where are you?"

"The abandoned mental asylum."

"Why are you... hello?" She was gone so I headed towards the abandoned asylum. I pushed the rusty door open and heard a scream. "Who's there? Where's my sister?"

"I'm here!"

I headed towards the room she was in, no one was there. All of a sudden, I felt someone pass me in hurry. "Bella, is that you? This better not be a prank!" I heard a strange, unfamiliar voice laughing in the background. The door slammed behind me. It was locked... The voice was getting closer...

JESSICA RYAN (12)

St Julie's Catholic High School, Woolton

WHO'S THERE?

My heart thumped, my lips twitched, I stood frozen with fear. Fearing what I'd entered, hearing crackles from the ceiling above me, I panicked. Where was I? How did I get here? Questions loomed around my head. I began to search for answers. It was empty downstairs, nothing in sight. I began to ascend up the stairs. I wandered around upstairs, cautious of who might be there. Suddenly, I began to hear the crackling again. "Hello?" No reply. The creaking of the floorboards, bangs on the walls, consistent laughs - who was there? Suddenly, the shadows lurking outside became visible...

EVIE ROBERTS (12)

St Julie's Catholic High School, Woolton

THE VICTORIAN HOUSE

Mum called down and said, "I'm going to the shops." I didn't like the thought of being left alone in a new Victorian house but shouldn't be acting like a baby - ghosts and spirits weren't real! Soon Mum left. For the first ten minutes, I was fine until I heard footsteps walking up the stairs, was it my imagination? I told myself everything was fine but then I heard banging. I couldn't help but look. When I looked there were three ghost people so I tried to run but I was grabbed by the arms. I screamed, "Someone help me..."

ROSIE ALI MOHAMMED (12)

St Julie's Catholic High School, Woolton

MY NIGHTMARE

The fog suffocated me, I couldn't see a thing. Walking for miles, finally I arrived but where was I? It seemed like an old dilapidated hospital. I had no choice but to venture in. I walked past the lonely, empty rooms, I could taste the fear building up inside me. Out of nowhere, I started hearing footsteps, noises and people screaming. Without thinking, I ran into a room. Paralysed with fear I could not move, my heart had stopped. "Take a breath!" I said to myself, trying to calm down. I turned around. There was my nightmare...

CHRISTELLE EVE BWAKA (12)
St Julie's Catholic High School, Woolton

THE ABANDONED SCHOOL

Who was that behind me? I crept down the abandoned school stairs, always peering behind me. A black figure kept emerging from the shadows, following my every step. I then sped into the bathroom, silently weeping on the phone for help. After ten minutes of waiting, I crawled to the door. I crawled back to the stairs and tiptoed down. Suddenly, the sound of heavy footsteps came closer as I sprinted to the door. Locked! I fiddled with the door when it fell silent. The only thing that was heard next to my echoing screams was a deep low laugh...

CERYS DAVIES (11)
St Julie's Catholic High School, Woolton

THE SCHOOL BATHROOM

The drips of the taps made my hair stand on end as I dried my hands. Why was I so scared? It was only the school bathroom! Nothing could happen to me, could it? As I flushed the tissue down the toilet, the water gurgled fiercely down the cracked pipes. The cubicle doors groaned and the humming behind the walls turned into roars.
Something was off. I looked in the mirror, black vines began to coil around it. The mirror began to crack. My eyes became distorted, my view whizzed and spiralled and there it was - the black figure...

SHONA SHAJI (12)
St Julie's Catholic High School, Woolton

The Asylum

It's time to tell my story... I was dared to enter a cold, abandoned mental asylum. As I walked in I saw an old-looking desk, I felt people staring at me but nobody was there. I ventured upstairs, my legs shaking, my hands ice-cold. I entered one of the cells, the bed lay there. I felt the urge to turn back but I couldn't. I heard laughter and a scream and fell into shock. I suddenly blacked out. I fell onto the cold ground and woke up and was in a hospital. How?

AMELIA BOYLE (12)
St Julie's Catholic High School, Woolton

Missing

Part of me is missing... One day, I had a weird feeling like something bad was going to happen and then something did... Me and my friend were sitting down, watching a movie when we heard a noise like a cat scratching on the door. My friend went to investigate. Moments later, I heard a scream. A scream which sounded like my friend's. From that moment he has never been found. This situation happened ten months ago and there's been no response since!

Amelia Jones (12)
St Julie's Catholic High School, Woolton

GONE

They'll never find me, I remember that day like it was yesterday! We went away on holiday and ended up in an old, haunted, dark house. This is where it all started. I can't bring myself to think about my family - Jack! Mum! Dad! Within a flash of light they were gone and I was left by myself with no one else. I haven't seen a human in decades. For all I know no one knows what happened to me or my family...

FILIPA CAIXINHA (12)

St Julie's Catholic High School, Woolton

Much Closer

Julian leapt from wet rooftop to wetter rooftop, unable to see. Fury fireballs exploded at his heels, singing his matted hair. (Ow! Hot!) Poison whipped past, missing him by inches (too close for comfort). He stumbled on, desperate to outrun the horrors behind him. Julian glanced back, catching sight of empty eyes staring back at him. Leathery wings spiked at the tip, jaws of death screaming otherworldly cries as they belched fireballs and spat acid. *They're closer,* he thought, *much closer!* Suddenly, the floor seemingly disappeared from under him. Too shocked to scream, he plummeted down to his horrible death.

Jason Wei (12)
The Bishop Of Llandaff CIW High School, Cardiff

Puppet Strings

There were practically puppet strings lodged into Darcy's shoulder blades, they were so sharp. There were even tiny slits in his back where the strings might have been, but that was more to do with his father's belt than Darcy's obedience. Tomorrow might be a little different but tonight wasn't over yet. Packing his suitcase for school the next day, Darcy's ears almost pricked up at the sound of his father's clicks and whistling; the same used with hunting dogs. The puppeteer was picking up the strings to play with the fifteen-year-old once again...

POLLY HOADE (13)
The Bishop Of Llandaff CIW High School, Cardiff

HOUSE OF THE DEAD

Knock, knock. No one answered. I looked over to my friend. "Let's go in the door." It creaked open and an immense fear hit me. "Do you feel that?"
"No."
This skinless man appeared.
"Argh!"
"Did you see that?"
"Yes and whatever it is it's not friendly or alone!"
Thud!
"Tim, where are you?" The knocking on the window sent a shiver down my spine. "Tim, this is not a time for jokes." I started banging on the door. "Let me out, please." I heard steps down the stairs.
"Join us, join us!"
"Please leave me alone..."

DANIEL DANTAS SA (11)
The Gatwick School, Crawley

THE OCTOBER NIGHTMARE

It was a dark night in late October, Emma, Charlie and Isabel stood frozen outside the Count's old house. People in the town said it was guarded to this day. "Go on then," said Charlie, while pushing Emma forward.

"Can't back out now!" said Isabel.

Emma stepped up to the door and knocked... Nothing happened. "See, there's nothing to be scared of!" yelled Emma, while shaking. As she turned around to go, the haunted mansion doors flung open and a cold, dirty hand grabbed Emma. The doors closed and the last thing Isabel and Charlie heard was Emma's scream...

CARYS CRESSWELL (12)

The Gatwick School, Crawley

ARE YOU THERE?

The fog crept along the floor. The sky was blacker than coal. The moon stared down at two innocent girls. "What's that noise?" muttered one of the girls. *Crack!* "Huh?" No answer. An echo repeated a scream. "Sam?" No answer... "Sam?" Charlie looked around for minutes, her heart felt as if it was going to jump from her chest. Goosebumps covered her spine. What was going on? She misplaced a step and tripped. Quickly grabbing onto a gravestone, she felt something wet. She lifted her hand, it was blood! She fell over, seeing her best friend's bloody body...

ISABELLA SEELIG (12)
The Gatwick School, Crawley

GONE

The flashlight went out, her phone battery must have died. It was not ideal for where they were. Alex and her friend Sam kept on walking. After about a mile more, Alex couldn't take the dark. "Have you got a torch?"

"No, left my phone at home but I see a phone booth." Alex put a pound in. *Ring, ring, ring...* "Hello, Dad. You need to pick us up now."

"Where are you?"

"I have no idea."

Whoosh! Scream! "I need to call you back. Sam, you there?"

A man walked up to her, the world went dark. Gone.

LEO HARWOOD-DUFFY (12)
The Gatwick School, Crawley

THE CUCKOO CLOCK

You hear a noise, a crash from the kitchen side. You call your words aloud with a sense of worry throughout. "Hello?" Your words echo through the house. You moved here recently during your travels. The clock ticks *tick-tock* and the thunder crashes. You move towards the living room, to check the problem. The screen of the TV clicks. The blurry lines enter the screen. The clock stops, you inspect the problem. The bird pops out - *squawk!* You jump, falling on your back, seeing a figure in the darkness. then it goes pitch-black. Then noise: *tick-tock...*

ELISE GRACE-HILLS (13)

The Gatwick School, Crawley

S.A.M

The door creaked shut. I looked around for Sam, he'd disappeared. The empty school corridors were unusual to walk through. The light suddenly flickered on and off, changing nothing except a mysterious red circle flashing ahead. Something moved behind me. I turned around, nothing. A doll suddenly appeared in front of me. Sam stepped out of a classroom, a long line of red pouring from his eyes. A guttural scream exited his lips and his eyes popped with a deafening noise. A circle engulfed him. It was a pentagram. Suddenly, nothing. I woke with a start, a doll lay near.

HARRISON JAMES BAMFORTH (11)
The Gatwick School, Crawley

THE GHOST VIRUS

Suddenly, *dong!* The clock struck twelve o'clock. We had no choice but to run. The ghost with the virus was touching people in the streets of my city. When you got it you died instantly. Suddenly the ghost gracefully cut open a dead person lying on the floor. My sister Maddie whispered, "We need to go, follow me!"
We ran over the grand bridge as I sobbed, "Where is Mum?" My sister ran into the ghost, I then decided to drag her with me. She slowed me down but I didn't care. Suddenly the ghost grabbed me. Goodnight lovely world!

ELEANOR ALLARD (12)
The Gatwick School, Crawley

Do Not Enter

One day, Poppy and Sky were wandering the streets when suddenly they both saw a haunted house. Sky really wanted to check it out but Poppy was a bit scared. Sky was saying to Poppy, "It will be fine, don't worry!" They both went up to the front door together. Sky opened the door and then they walked inside. Suddenly the door slammed behind them and Poppy started screaming because she was terrified. Sky started exploring when she realised there must be a ghost in the house. They got scared and ran out the back door...

"Do not enter!"

Casey Burgar (13)

The Gatwick School, Crawley

DARE TO COME IN

Don't you dare enter the circle of trees. What's waiting there you will see. As you walk through the circle of trees, you see a mansion. Debating whether to go in or not, your hand shakes as you push open the door...

"Help me!"

"What was that?" you tremble as you crawl up the rotten stairs. You want to go back but can't leave without the secret it holds. You hear the rustling of bushes outside the window. What you see is what you would never even dream of... Remember, you never know how much time there could be left!

HOPE PHELPS (12)

The Gatwick School, Crawley

The Monster

I came home from school all exhausted but prepared for the monster. Knowing what would happen I hid in my wardrobe with the house phone in case got too bad. He opened the front door, the sound of silence killed me until the monster giggled and shouted, "I know you're in here!" He giggled again. The monster, eager to hurt me, opened the bedroom door. My mind was playing tricks on me as he dropped his empty beer. The glass flew everywhere. Emotions flying and his hand clutching the wardrobe... The monster was my dad who didn't even love me...

KERYS BARROW (11)
The Gatwick School, Crawley

Walking Home

As the sun waved goodbye, the moon lurked towards the Earth, looking down on its prey. I could feel a mild chill filling my stomach and goosebumps filling my spine. It was just a walk from school, surely it wasn't that terrifying! Maybe I shouldn't have gone to that after school club because I had to walk alone at sunset, with all mankind silently dozing away with the warm company of their family. I felt a slight, sharp tap on my shoulder. I glanced over but no sign of anyone. A glooming shadow was standing upright, someone was following me...

Roheyatou Jagana (12)

The Gatwick School, Crawley

Cold Cottage And The Strange Figure

The man looked into the cold, dark, ghost-like cottage. He took two steps towards the cold cottage and got chills all the way down his spine and body. He kept on walking and ignored the cold, unholy welcome he received. The house was simple and had odd-looking windows, it was a crooked house and had many plants and leaves growing from previous gardens. He noticed a black, gloomy, scary figure in his window as he tried to wave to the strange man-like figure it vanished into the darkness. The man continued on to the cold house. Beware the demons...

Xanthe Valentine (14)
The Gatwick School, Crawley

HEARTBROKEN

As the sun bowed down to the moon, it looked as horrifying as I imagined. I crept up to the mansion and opened the creaking door as a colony of bats stormed out of the spine-chilling house, as I tried to turn my flashlight on but failed, luckily I had my phone on me so it was fine. As I started searching I heard a creaking noise upstairs. Panicking, I shouted lightly, "Hello?" As soon as I said that, three or four people came rushing down the stairs in horror. Suddenly, they stopped and one of them said creepily, "Hello..."

HARRY SMITH (13)

The Gatwick School, Crawley

THE TALE OF DAISY HITCHCOCK

My breathing got louder and louder, harder and harder and I got even more anxious. The sound of little children laughing came along with me and didn't stop. I was horrified to the core of my heart. I saw a house coming up, it was old and creepy but it was the only choice I had. I shut the door behind and yelled, "Hello, is anyone there?" No reply.
I kept asking when there was a deafening scream, "Run!" It came from nowhere. I heard "Boo!" in my ear and felt a hand on my shoulder. I wasn't seen again.

DAISY HITCHCOCK (13)
The Gatwick School, Crawley

THE DREAM OF HORROR

There was blood everywhere, floorboards creaked in the darkness. I walked to the door. It opened with a bony hand covered in blood. As I walked in, I heard rattles. Was it really rattlesnakes? One bite and dead! Up the rotten stairs, I found bones everywhere, puddles of dripping blood and livers. I slipped on them. As I continued my journey through the haunted house, more piles of bones were stacked. I heard footsteps coming towards me. Was it a monster? It was just a man. He held a chainsaw and vroom went the chainsaw... I woke up in fright!

PAIGE SMITH (11)

The Gatwick School, Crawley

DON'T LOOK UP

Margaret felt every spindle of grass brush her boots as she began to ascend up the steps. One step, two steps... She stopped dead at the door, her hand gripped hold of the handle, twisting it. A small bell rang and she knew she was at her dead grandma's house. It was drop-dead silent, other than the squeak of the wood door. She turned her head. "Grandma?" she choked. He grandma's corpse hung from the small chandelier, maggots crawling from her eyes like dried tears. On her arm a message was cut: *Don't look up!*

PAIGE NEWMAN (12)
The Gatwick School, Crawley

THE DANGER DOOR

I heard a deafening shriek, my spine shivered as I made my way towards an ordinary door which had a bright yellow danger sign on it and, of course, I turned the handle and opened it. Suddenly the room filled with a foggy mist, I couldn't see anything. My heart was pumping rapidly. The mist cleared slowly and a cracked and rotten staircase appeared. It seemed to be never-ending. I stepped onto the stairs and continuously climbed up. On my way up I saw a shadowy figure follow me and bright shiny eyes were staring through my soul...

AMBERJEET PANESAR (12)

The Gatwick School, Crawley

ALONE

I opened my eyes, it was dark, so dark. I tried to stand, I couldn't. My body was stiff, cold. I began to panic, why was I here? I could feel something dripping down my face. It was warm. What was I doing? My head was screaming in pain. What happened? I heard something scuttling past me, was it a rat? The chains that tied me down were tight around my wrists. I struggled but they wouldn't come loose. I felt the gentle feeling of fingertips brush against my shoulder. My heart was pounding as I realised I wasn't alone...

ANNIE MAE HITCHCOCK (15)

The Gatwick School, Crawley

MURDER

Blood splattered down the walls. The victim lay lifeless on the cold, hard floor. The murderer stood against the crimson wall. he sat down and pulled out a knife. He sharpened it. the knife flew through the air, hitting the statue and shattering it into pieces. He picked up a shard of glass then there was a knock. The clock struck 12. Dragging his victim to the side, he cut off his head to join his family who were also hanging on the walls. He then returned to his place behind the pillar, waiting for his next victim to arrive...

KATIE WILLIMOTT (12)
The Gatwick School, Crawley

Drip, Drip, Drip

I walked over the old, broken bridge, not knowing what horror awaited me. I approached the old house, the door handle covered in blood. I opened the door, covering my hand with the blood. I walked through the dark corridor, opened the door on the left, every inch of it covered in spiders. As I walked in I looked around and dead bodies were all up the walls. Their throats slit - *drip, drip, drip* the blood went. One girl in the middle, bleeding from her wrists. Thick, dark, red blood. I heard a scream and stepped back...

Jessica Gurr (15)

The Gatwick School, Crawley

Pentagrams

The silence nearly killed me. Whenever I turned back there was nobody behind me. There were shivers going around my body and it felt like someone was breathing down my neck. Late at night and walking home alone, I stopped to lean against a door. Then it opened, nothing was there except spiders and cobwebs. A pentagram was on the floor, set alight. Spikes lay and voices were heard. Soon enough I began to think I wasn't alone. Luckily, a cupboard was behind me so I leapt into it. Something was here with me. I would find it...

Louise Cannon (11)

The Gatwick School, Crawley

SOMEONE HELP ME, I'M STRANDED

Whooshing sounds of footsteps coming from behind the door of the house, I walked in. There was a big bang as the door slammed behind me. I looked up to see a huge, rotting, stained staircase, that is when I knew I needed to go. I ran to the door but it wouldn't open. Out of nowhere, something unhuman grabbed me from behind. Struggling, screaming, it took me to the stairs and held me by the bannister, swinging me back and forth. Nothing in the house was stable. I was bound to die. The creature said nothing, just howled...

CHENAI VUSANI (15)
The Gatwick School, Crawley

THE MAN

I walked towards the house, my heart squeezed inside me, my goosebumps getting stronger and stronger with every step I took. I got to the bloody door, my heart was racing by now. Every breath I took I felt as if it was my last. I had no other option so I crept in. I walked towards the curtains, the wind brushed against my face then suddenly a door banged shut and my body froze. I tried getting away but couldn't move. The sound of someone walking down the stairs was getting louder and louder but then there he was...

ZAHRA MAHMOOD (15)

The Gatwick School, Crawley

THE HALLWAY OF DEATH

Phill was walking across a deep, pitch-black hallway. He felt like monsters were lurking all around him. When he suddenly saw light, he ran towards it. That was a big mistake. He ran straight into a bright glowing beast that had never been seen before. He ran away immediately and screamed. He kept running and running until he met a dead end. He saw an open vent and saw a stack of chairs. He climbed the chairs to the vent and escaped. He crawled around in the vents. Then he heard heavy breathing. He knew he would die...

CAITLIN TRIGWELL (12)
The Gatwick School, Crawley

VERTEBRAE FREEZER

The air got colder. I stuttered over to the colossal door, the skulls on it stared at me, lifeless. I pushed the big door with all my strength and was greeted to a long, cold staircase. I tried to turn on the lights to no avail. Thoughts streamed through my mind, I should leave. Why was I here? I clumsily fumbled for the door but it was locked. My breathing sped up, I felt cold. I couldn't leave again. I looked up at the staircase and saw something. I went cold as it approached me. My mind went completely frozen...

THOMAS STAGG (14)
The Gatwick School, Crawley

Missing

Creepy voices spoke to me like I was the chosen one, encouraging me to keep walking, that I would live. I did as I was told. The house had crimson writing warning not to come near or death would come! As gruesome as it was, I went in... Hours before I was found, I saw a younger girl screaming for help. I sprinted as fast as I could towards her. I untangled her, realising who she was - my little sister, lost almost a year before I found her! I screamed at her, "Run!" We sprinted quickly out of the house...

Pippa Watts (12)

The Gatwick School, Crawley

DOCTORS

It was a cold spring night, I was on my home from work. I had to clean out the unknown coffin that was buried last week but there was something strange about it - it was empty! On my way home, warm air ran down my neck. I quickly looked to one side and saw nothing. Laughter filled the air. The clouds started to part around me, opening a bright darkness, screaming and screaming. Big hands grabbed me, I shut my eyes tight and reopened them to a bright white light. I looked around, doctors pinned me down, laughing...

ROCHELLE BARROW (15)

The Gatwick School, Crawley

Dark Falling

I wandered through the dark woods, terrified. Where was I? How was I supposed to get home? Suddenly I came to a halt. Something was following me. I started taking unexpected twists and turns, hoping to lose them or it. I was disappointed. It seemed to know my every move. My heart in my throat, I began to run. I ran for what felt like forever and then suddenly I fell. I didn't know what had happened but I was definitely falling. I looked up, or it could have been down. Darkness. It was all I would ever see...

Lucy Munday (12)

The Gatwick School, Crawley

Feels Like I'm Being Watched

The pathway was filled with mud. As I walked up to the gloomy house I hesitantly opened the door. The stairs were tarnished and slowly breaking, I decided to climb up what was left of them. There was a long and eerie hallway, pictures were hung up along the wall. There were ten doors, I tried to open the door closest to me but it was locked. The rest of the doors were too but I hadn't tried the last one yet. I felt like I was being watched. I slowly and cautiously opened the cracked, worn and dirty door...

AAMANI PAREKH (14)
The Gatwick School, Crawley

Shell-Shocked

I was aghast when I saw the house, I thought it was a luxurious house! What was in it? Why did it look so suspicious? The contamination was racing through my spine, preventing me from inhaling any fresh air. As I was looking in the graveyard, I was mesmerised by the liveliness of the grave. Here I was, in the spine-shivering house. The red-eyed bats scattered from the floor, screeching and shoving their way out. I opened the creaking door, my heart was pounding like the heart of a lion. I opened the closet...

David Mihai (13)
The Gatwick School, Crawley

ENTERING

Walking through the dry, barren land, you are trying to find a place to rest. In the distance, you see the house. Apparently, if you step over the threshold bad things will happen to you and around you but you don't believe in ghosts and you enter. You open the door, you get a chill down your spine, inside is colder than outside. Upstairs you hear the creak of a floorboard and feel like someone is watching you. You see something that looks like a moving rocking chair... It stops moving and you see him...

ELOISE MAAN (13)

The Gatwick School, Crawley

THE HUMAN EATER

I walked down the dark narrow hallway of an abandoned house, finding a shadow on a wall. A shape of a person was walking away from me. Then automatically the lights flickered on. Then I found a three-foot pile of lifeless dead bodies with intestines, lungs and other organs splattered all over the pathway. I backed away in fear to see dead children and adults assembled in a huge pile. My stomach growled as I looked out of the corner of my eye... fresh bright red organs on the floor. Then I devoured it all...

KIMORA KANJANDA (11)
The Gatwick School, Crawley

PAIN

I lurk between the shadows. The moon casting light over the forest. A dead fox lies beneath an old oak tree. I place my hand on the cold, rough bark. Fog fills the air. I scrape my hand on the bark. Crimson-red blood trickles out of my hand. I wipe my hand on my ripped clothes. I cry in desperate pain. My eyes fill with tears. After the blood dries I pick it. The pain swells in my fingers. A raven is perched high on a branch. It is pitch-black. I hear loud piercing footsteps. Something is hunting me...

JESSICA MARY-ANNE COOKE (11)
The Gatwick School, Crawley

SPINE CHILLERS 2020 - FROM THE SHADOWS

A Room I Remember

A chill shoots up my spine as I tread along unforgiving steps and I watch as the moon sneers its crescent smile. As I move forward in the maze, I know too well, I look around to see a jungle of cobwebs. Slowly, the doors that line the corridors either side of me become sparse and I reach a door taller and stronger than the rest. Anxiety numbs my mind from a static humming sound and my nose becomes oblivious to a horrible stench as I reach for the handle. What do I find? My body, dead on the ground...

Carolina Santana (14)
The Gatwick School, Crawley

WALKING HOME

My phone was dead. I could not contact my parents. I started walking home and I took a shortcut. Then out of the corner of my eye, I saw a shadow. My senses heightened, I felt goosebumps prick my skin and I could hear footsteps approaching. My heart wanted to jump right out of its cage. I saw a river ahead. Before I knew it, I was in the river, swimming for my life. I relaxed thinking I was safe but standing before me was a man with a menacing smile, holding out his hands. What should I do now...?

JESSICA FIYINFOLUWA FAWOLE (13)
The Gatwick School, Crawley

A LETTER FROM A VAMPIRE

Dear Reader,

You haven't got much time left. You are the only one who can see this letter because the house you live in once belonged to me. I am coming back to where I have always belonged and nothing is stopping me because now I have the power I always wanted to have. A long time ago a fairy fell in love with me but I never loved her back so she put a spell on me and turned me into a vampire. She locked me up for five hundred years. Remember I'm coming!

From

Gilbert Smith

MANUELA RAIMUNDO (12)

The Gatwick School, Crawley

THE GREAT FLOOD

I awoke after a sudden dream. I tumbled out of bed to the noise of creaky floorboards and screams coming from outside. I peered out of my window. The view I had was jaw-dropping blood and fear on people's faces. I had to act... I grabbed my shotgun and opened up a window. I stuck the barrel of my gun just out of the window and took a shot. The crack of the bullet skimmed across the city then the creatures ran to my house. I slammed the window but they were coming. I was scared. Please help!

HARRY FEILD (14)

The Gatwick School, Crawley

The Theme Park

Me and my friend decided to go to a theme park as it was going to stay sunny for the rest of the day. We got in the car and put the radio on. Finally, we got there. It was quiet. It felt like a schoolday but it wasn't. We went on all the rides twice but this strange dirty man followed us on all the rides. My friend was hungry so went to get food. It was scary. That strange man was serving us. He stared and didn't look away. My heart was pounding. He leaned closer... "Argh!"

Harriet Watts (11)
The Gatwick School, Crawley

A Raptor's Claw

My heart was racing faster than a rabbit as I darted towards the entrance to the tree house. The dangling ladder swayed as the wind shoved it. I got a grasp on the ladder and started to climb as it pounced trying to stop me. Its claws scraped my calf and pulled. the pain loosened my grip as I slipped down but its claw on my leg dug deeper. The next thing I knew, its icy-cold breath made me shiver. That was the last of my leg! The next thing I knew, I heard a bang and the creature fell...

Cole Scott (13)
The Gatwick School, Crawley

OLD HOLLOW WOOD HOUSE

As I walked past the creaky gate I tripped on a stone, it was a creepy little thing. It had a scary demon-like face. The door was dirty and had piles of mud stuck to it as well as some dents and two big lion-faced doorbells. I knocked the one closest to me, the right one. It was two loud knocks and with that it opened, but no one was there... I looked around and saw one big painting that was of an old lady. As I took a closer look, the painting tore and a figure stared at me...

JAMES RUBY (13)
The Gatwick School, Crawley

Foggy Prank Day

Once again I was home and it was getting foggy. I wanted to go out to play but it was too foggy. All of a sudden I got a cold chill down my back. It was getting dark and all of a sudden I got hit... Nothing was in my room, I was getting scared. It was about two hours later and everything had gone... There was silence. All of a sudden, a bloody hand scraped against my window like it was a bear paw. Then my door slammed shut. Suddenly my mum knocked on the window. Pranked!

ROSE WALLER (12)

The Gatwick School, Crawley

THE CLEARING IN THE WOODS

One day I was walking through the woods when I came to a clearing. At first I thought nothing of it until I looked up and saw a spooky house leaning on a hill with a gravestone outside. As I wandered up to the house I decided to see if anyone was in or not. I walked up the steps of the house and knocked on the door. I waited about two minutes for someone to answer but they didn't. I tried the door handle but it was locked. What should I do? Was there another way...?

TILLY ASTLEY (11)
The Gatwick School, Crawley

The Haunted House

I was at the park when suddenly I came across a scary house. I wanted to see what was inside so I went in. The door opened by broke right after. I walked in but there wasn't much furniture, the only thing that was in the house was a TV. The TV started to play a scary video from a scary movie. I started to run away and I saw a room. There was a bed and it looked like there was a person in the bed. Was there? I started to take the covers off and it grabbed me...

Tatiana Almeida (13)
The Gatwick School, Crawley

THE KRAKEN

It was a normal day after school and I was on my way home with my sister and my friend. We were walking the normal way home and my friend said he knew a shortcut so we went with him. He took us through some bizarre alleys but this last one was long and scary. All of a sudden, a crack of thunder struck and there was a loud crack in the sky. Me and my sister jumped and my friend had disappeared but me and my sister decided to keep going. Then a Kraken appeared...

ALEX WILLIAMS (15)
The Gatwick School, Crawley

DROPPED

I walked in and there was a big bang as the door slammed behind me. I looked up to see a huge rotting staircase in front of me that was when I knew I shouldn't be in the house. I tried to escape but it was like it was bolted shut multiple times. I tried to scream for help when something unhuman-like grabbed me from behind and began to drag me upstairs by my collar. When I got to the top, it held me over the bannister, swinging me back and forth...

NATASHA EAMES (15)

The Gatwick School, Crawley

I HAVE AN ADMIRER

I was about ten when it happened, I was packing for a camping trip in a week. I was the middle of summer so I had my window open. I turned around to get a pair of shorts, when I turned back I saw a man trying to get in my room. I screamed and my dad came in and the man left. He came back four times a week so we moved to a ramshackle house and one day, I awoke to the man at the door and I could see the wall through him. Then he vanished forever.

CHRISTOPHER MILES (15)

The Gatwick School, Crawley

Est.1991

YOUNG WRITERS
INFORMATION

We hope you have enjoyed reading this book – and that you will continue to in the coming years.

If you're a young writer who enjoys reading and creative writing, or the parent of an enthusiastic poet or story writer, do visit our website www.youngwriters.co.uk. Here you will find free competitions, workshops and games, as well as recommended reads, a poetry glossary and our blog.

If you would like to order further copies of this book, or any of our other titles, then please give us a call or visit **www.youngwriters.co.uk.**

Young Writers
Remus House
Coltsfoot Drive
Peterborough
PE2 9BF
(01733) 890066 / 898110
info@youngwriters.co.uk